P9-DEK-539

A NEW CAMFIELD NOVEL OF LOVE

BARBARA CARTLAND

Only a Dream

JOVE BOOKS, NEW YORK

ONLY A DREAM

A Jove Book/published by arrangement with
the author

PRINTING HISTORY
Jove edition / October 1988

ISBN: 0-515-09754-3

Jove Books are published by The Berkley Publishing Group,
200 Madison Avenue, New York, New York 10016.
The name "JOVE" and the "J" logo
are trademarks belonging to Jove Publications, Inc.

PRINTED IN THE UNITED STATES OF AMERICA

10 9 8 7 6 5 4 3 2 1

Camfield Place,
Hatfield
Hertfordshire,
England

Dearest Reader,

Camfield Novels of Love mark a very exciting era of my books with Jove. They have already published nearly two hundred of my titles since they became my first publisher in America, and now all my original paperback romances in the future will be published exclusively by them.

As you already know, Camfield Place in Hertfordshire is my home, which originally existed in 1275, but was rebuilt in 1867 by the grandfather of Beatrix Potter.

It was here in this lovely house, with the best view in the county, that she wrote *The Tale of Peter Rabbit*. Mr. McGregor's garden is exactly as she described it. The door in the wall that the fat little rabbit could not squeeze underneath and the goldfish pool where the white cat sat twitching its tail are still there.

I had Camfield Place blessed when I came here in 1950 and was so happy with my husband until he died, and now with my children and grandchildren, that I know the atmosphere is filled with love and we have all been very lucky.

It is easy here to write of love and I know you will enjoy the Camfield Novels of Love. Their plots are definitely exciting and the covers very romantic. They come to you, like all my books, with love.

Bless you,

CAMFIELD NOVELS OF LOVE

by Barbara Cartland

Other books by Barbara Cartland

Only a Dream

"Where am I . . . to go?" Isla asked.

There was silence, and after a moment the Marquis said: "I should be delighted to have you as my guest."

He chose his words carefully and tried not to let his real feelings show in his voice.

"I want you to give us both time to find a solution to your problem. Nothing must be done in a hurry."

He thought as he spoke that when she knew him better, she might fall in love with him the same way he had fallen in love with her.

Then he almost laughed at his own thoughts.

Could he really be so unsure of himself, he who had been pursued, enticed, and seduced by almost every beautiful woman he had met? . . .

A Camfield Novel of Love
by Barbara Cartland

———

"Barbara Cartland's novels are all distinguished by their intelligence, good sense, and good nature . . ."
— ROMANTIC TIMES

"Who could give better advice on how to keep your romance going strong than the world's most famous romance novelist, Barbara Cartland?"
— THE STAR

Author's Note

THE Music Hall actually goes back to mediaeval times. In the Dark Ages tumblers and musicians diverted the Car-Lords in their strong-holds, while minstrels either sang or recited the news of their exploits to the common people.

The Elizabethans were entertainment-minded; their toughness and enterprise was tempered by a love of wit and beauty.

It was not until 1860 that the first professional female singer appeared at the more respectable song-and-dance Supper-Rooms in Covent Garden.

The first real Music Hall was Charles Morton's New Canterbury, which opened in London in 1854. Fifteen hundred enthusiasts could eat, drink, and make merry beneath the enormous gas-lit chandeliers.

Seven years later, Morton built himself the Oxford, then transformed the decrepit Old Mogul Theatre at Cambridge Circus into the Palace, the most stylish of Metropolitan Music Halls.

This story is about the Oxford, which was open every evening and on Saturday afternoons, and was exceedingly popular for many years.

The premises were later acquired by John Lyons and were transformed into the Oxford Street Corner House.

chapter one

1867

ISLA heard a knock on the front-door.

Quickly putting down the bowl in which she was preparing supper, she ran into the hall.

She knew from the way the person outside had knocked that it was her father.

She pulled open the door and he walked in.

With his top-hat at an angle, he looked exceedingly smart, but she knew with a sinking of her heart that he had been drinking.

"You are back, Papa!" she exclaimed. "I was afraid you might be late."

"It is not surprising that I am," he replied sharply.

He put his top-hat down on a chair and moved towards the Sitting-Room.

The house was tiny and it made Keegan Kenway look

taller and more broad-shouldered than he actually was.

At the same time, he was an exceedingly good-looking man.

He was so good-looking that the crowds outside the stage-door cheered when he appeared, and his admirers never failed to turn up whenever he was performing.

He was, however, not as young as he used to be.

Only Isla knew how much he had deteriorated since her mother had died a little over a year ago.

He had seldom had too much to drink when she was alive, even though it was difficult to be abstemious in the world of the Theatre.

There was always somebody celebrating a success, or drinking because they were depressed.

Now, nearly every evening when Keegan Kenway came home, he was slightly unsteady on his feet, and slurring his words.

Then Isla knew she would have to help him up to bed.

Otherwise he would sit with his head in his hands, the tears rolling down his cheeks as he told her how much he missed her mother.

That was true, but although she loved him, she could not help feeling it was an over-exaggerated expression of self-pity.

It was not only because he was so unhappy, but also because he had drunk too much.

Now, as he flung himself down in an armchair in the Sitting-Room, she said brightly in a tone which was meant to cheer him up:

"Supper will be ready in a few minutes, and I am sure you are hungry."

She glanced at the clock as she spoke and saw that it was fifteen minutes past midnight.

This meant, since the Theatre usually closed before

2

eleven, that he had been drinking with one of his cronies before coming home.

Sometimes he went out to supper with friends.

Then he was always insistent that she should go to bed early and on no account come downstairs when she heard him arrive home.

In the last few months, however, she had been aware that it was often three or four o'clock in the morning before he returned.

He would then sleep late the next morning and she would creep about the house so as not to wake him.

Now, even as she spoke and would have returned to the kitchen, something stopped her.

It was perhaps her father's attitude, or the expression on his face, which was not his usual one when he was missing her mother.

It was somehow different.

She ran to his side to kneel down by his chair.

"What is the matter, Papa?" she asked.

"I have lost my chance of being able to perform for the Benefit tomorrow evening," he answered, "and God knows, I need the money!"

"But why? What has happened?"

It flashed through her mind that he had been sacked, but that was impossible.

She was well aware how popular her father had become since he had given up performing in what was called the "Legitimate" Theatre.

Instead, he had joined Charles Morton's New Canterbury Music Hall, which had opened in Lamberth thirteen years before.

Her mother, however, had been rather shocked by his decision.

She had never visited a Music Hall and certainly had not allowed Isla to enter one.

The money, however, was good, and Keegan Kenway, from being no more than a fairly well-known actor had become almost overnight what was known as a *Lion Comique*.

The term, Isla was aware, meant "heavy swell."

Dressed in the smartest fashion, complete with waxed moustache, silk hat, and cane, he was the talk of London.

The songs he sang, and he had a very good voice, were whistled by every errand-boy, and the younger actors in the Theatre all tried to copy his appearance.

After some years at the New Canterbury, Keegan Kenway had moved to the Oxford Music Hall, which had been built in Oxford Street in 1861.

His performance there was acclaimed by the newspapers, and there was no doubt he was now "a draw" which the owner, Charles Morton, appreciated.

Nevertheless, Keegan Kenway seemed to be always in debt, and Isla worried, as her mother had done, as to how they could pay their bills.

There was also the wages of the woman who came in daily to scrub the kitchen-floor.

Isla had always known her father was generous, but he had never been so overwhelmingly generous to his friends when her mother was alive as he was after her death.

In fact, Isla had meant to ask him for money when he came home that night.

The Butcher had been surly when she shopped earlier in the day and asked for what she bought to go on their account.

The Fishmonger had said he was a poor man, with his own commitments to meet.

The shopkeepers could not imagine that anyone as

famous as her father was ever short of money or came home night after night with empty pockets.

If Isla protested, he would always answer:

"I only stood the boys a drink! After all, they are my closest friends!" or "There is a girl in the Theatre who is literally 'down on her uppers.' She had been left in the lurch by somebody she trusted. I had to help her!"

Money slipped through Keegan Kenway's fingers not so much like water as like champagne.

This was somehow appropriate, since he sang songs that made the newcomers to London believe that "the streets were paved with gold," and no "man-about-town" would even drink anything but "bubbly."

But whatever it was that Keegan Kenway drank off-stage was making his dark eyes, which had beguiled so many of the women in his audience, blood-shot.

His voice, too, was much thicker than it had been, and there was a suspicious slackening in the line of his chin.

He was still exceedingly handsome.

But at forty-eight he did not look the same Adonis he had been twenty years earlier, when he had married her mother.

"What has happened, Papa?" Isla asked anxiously. "Why can you not be in the Benefit?"

She had been counting on the Benefit.

These were performances which took place frequently at most Theatres to supplement the salaries of the performers.

The performers in the Music Halls did not earn as much as the actors and actresses at Drury Lane or Covent Garden because it had to be divided among many more of them.

Nevertheless, what her father would have received would have been extremely welcome, and there was a note almost of despair in Isla's voice as she said softly:

"Tell me . . . about it . . . Papa."

"Letty Liston collapsed after the performance tonight and the Doctor insisted she should go to Hospital!"

"Oh, Papa, how terrible!"

Isla knew exactly what this meant.

Although she had never seen Letty Liston, she knew she was very attractive and a big success in the present Show at the Oxford when she appeared as a woman in a picture.

Dressed in a large white crinoline with a wreath on her fair hair, she sat in a frame on an almost dark stage.

Then her father would come swaggering, supposedly staggering home after a party.

Wearing his top-hat at an angle and twisting his cane, he was the handsome, raffish "Smart Johnny" whom all the girls loved.

He would look up at the picture.

Then in his deep baritone voice, which could still make the heart of any woman who listened to him flitter, he would beg her to dance with him.

Surprisingly the picture would "come to life," Letty Liston would step down on to the stage, her father would put his arms around her, and they would Waltz round and round.

As he stopped, held her close, and was about to kiss her, the curtains would close.

Then they opened again, and Letty was back in the picture frame.

It was then, in a voice that brought tears to the eyes of all who listened to him, that Keegan Kenway would sing "It Was Only a Dream."

It was a very pretty, sentimental song, and because his voice, which had been magnificent, still retained much of its earlier tone, the Theatre would be absolutely silent.

The diners and the drinkers never moved until he had finished.

In all her eighteen years, Isla had not seen him on the stage, but she had read the notices in the newspapers and he practised the song at home.

She would play the piano and, although she knew the song by heart, it was easy to understand how much more effective it was when he exerted himself in the Theatre.

For Keegan Kenway it was the triumphant moment of the evening.

Not to perform at the Benefit, Isla knew, would disappoint not only him, but all those who had paid to come to see him.

"Surely it would not be difficult to find somebody to take Letty's place?" she asked.

He laughed, and it was not a sound of amusement.

"The only women I could get at this late hour," he said, "are the 'has beens' who hang about the Theatrical Agents hoping for a 'walk on' part."

"Then what can you do, Papa? We need the money!"

"Do you suppose I am not aware of that?" her father asked savagely. "And I signed an IOU for George Vance this afternoon."

"Oh, no, Papa!"

"I could not refuse the Chap."

"But . . . what will happen to us . . . Papa if you . . . give all . . . your money away?"

There was silence.

Then, as if she felt she must make an effort to cheer him up, she said:

"Come and have some supper. Perhaps you will be able to think of something after you have eaten."

"Give me a drink first."

"No . . . Papa. You know it is bad for you, and Mama always made you have something to eat when you came off the stage."

Isla got up from the floor and, taking her father's hand in hers, pulled him to his feet.

He struggled up with what she knew was an effort and walked with her across the room.

He brushed his shoulder awkwardly against the door-frame as he passed through it.

She did not say anything but led him into the Dining-Room on the other side of the hall.

As he sat down in his chair, she ran to bring in the soup, which she had kept warm on the stove.

She had cooked it very carefully as her mother had taught her, and it was nourishing as well as well flavoured.

As her father started to eat, she told herself things could not be as bad as they appeared.

Keegan Kenway finished the soup.

By the time Isla had brought in a steak, which was just as he liked it, he had got a bottle of whisky out of the cupboard.

One glance at the glass by his side told Isla there was very little soda with it.

She made no comment, but when he had drunk down the whisky and looked at the steak, he demanded a glass of claret.

"Red wine with red meat," he said. "That is the rule. There is some claret left which I brought home last week."

"Only half a bottle, Papa," Isla said. "You drank a good deal of it last night."

"I expect there is more where that came from!" Keegan Kenway replied.

Isla knew he was thinking of the rich patrons of the Oxford who occupied the comfortable boxes and some-times sent him a case of wine.

They sent the ladies in the Show flowers and jewellery, but Isla knew her mother had often wished where Keegan

Kenway was concerned they would not be so generous.

The drink he received was the one thing he did not give away.

Isla brought the bottle of claret to the table and poured him out a glass, but he stopped her from putting the bottle back on the sideboard.

"I think you have had enough, Papa, and you know it will not do you any good."

"Nothing can be worse than the mess I am in at the moment," her father replied angrily. "What am I to do, Isla? What the Devil can I do?"

"I am sure you can find somebody to take Letty's place," Isla said confidently. "What about the pretty girls in the Show? The newspapers say they are the best-looking women in London!"

"That is true enough," her father replied, "but they have their own acts and will not take part in mine!"

"Why not?"

"Because when they are on the stage they want the applause for themselves, and do not want to share it with me."

"That seems rather selfish, when you do so much for them," Isla murmured.

She was well aware how much her father spent on the women in the Music Hall, but she was not quite certain why they were so expensive.

She only supposed that, when she found powder on his evening-clothes when she brushed them, they had been expressing their gratitude for the money he had given them.

It was strange he should be so generous to women because she was sure it was something that had never happened in her mother's lifetime.

He would say, if she questioned him, that the women were actresses who were "down on their luck," had "struck a bad patch," or were "hoping for better things tomorrow" —a tomorrow which never came.

Her father seemed to help them all.

She told herself that if he did not get a Benefit, he would have to borrow to keep the house going until the next one.

Keegan Kenway finished his supper and the bottle was empty.

"You should go to bed, Papa," Isla said.

"How can I sleep when I am worrying about tomorrow?" he asked irritably. "Give me another drink."

"There is no more . . . and you . . . have had . . . enough!"

For a moment she thought he was going to defy her.

Then slowly he got to his feet, and, holding on to the table, then to one of the chairs, he reached the door.

He did not say good night.

She heard him stumble up the stairs, go into the front bedroom he had shared with her mother, and slam the door behind him.

She wondered if she should go after him and help him out of his clothes.

Once or twice he had been so incapable that he had just thrown himself down on the bed and slept as he was.

Isla had then had the trouble of pressing his clothes until they looked smart enough for him to wear them again.

Then with a deep sigh she decided he was best left alone.

She carried the plates and cutlery into the kitchen, and, because she was tired, decided she would leave them in the sink and wash them up tomorrow.

She turned out the oil-lamps in the room they had been using and went up the stairs very softly.

She paused outside her father's door to see if she could hear him snoring.

There was, however, silence, and because she was worried, she opened the door very quietly.

As she suspected, he had not blown out the candles she had lit beside the bed just before he came home.

He had undressed, but his clothes were lying all over the floor.

She thought he must be asleep, and she walked on tiptoe into the room, picked up his coat and his stiff-fronted shirt, and put them on an armchair.

His black trousers and his waist-coat went on another.

Then, as she moved towards the bed to blow out the candles, she realised he was not asleep, but watching her.

"You are awake . . . Papa!" she said in a low voice.

"I was thinking you are very like your mother," her father answered, "and for a moment, when you came in, I thought she had come . . . back."

The pain in his voice was unmistakable, and Isla said gently:

"I know that wherever she is, Papa, she is thinking of you and loving you."

She put her hand over his as it lay outside the sheet and said:

"I am sure she will help us, and perhaps think of a solution to our problem."

Her father looked at her with what she thought were bleary eyes.

The light from the candle made her hair very golden, and it haloed her small, pointed face.

"You are lovely, very lovely!" he said in a thick voice. "Why should you not take Letty's place? You are far prettier than she is!"

Isla stared at him in astonishment.

Then, as she was about to reply, she realised he had shut

his eyes and, as if he had found a solution to what was worrying him, had fallen asleep.

For some seconds she stood just looking at him.

Then she blew out the lights and, leaving the room, shut the door very quietly.

In her own bedroom Isla thought it was a very strange thing for her father to have said.

Although, of course, he did not mean it, it was something, if she could do it, that would enable him to claim his share in the Benefit.

Then she laughed at the idea as being quite ridiculous.

Ever since she could remember, her mother had forbidden her to have anything to do with the theatrical side of her father's life.

She had been to the Theatre, but not to see him.

Instead, her mother had taken her to see *A Midsummer Night's Dream*, *King Lear*, and *Hamlet*.

She had also seen *The Silver King*, a great melodrama acted by Wilfred Barrett—the great romantic actor.

She watched him in *Hamlet* and in a play called *Junius* written by Bulwer-Lytton, which was a failure.

Last year Wilfred Barrett had presented and acted *Clito* —a tragedy set in Athens in 500 B.C.

It was not a financial success but an artistic one.

It made Isla know what she wanted of life, the noble and spiritual love which lifted those who found it up to the stars.

Strangely, it was an absolute rule that she should never see her father perform.

What was more, she was not even allowed to be known as an actor's daughter.

Her mother, by some means she had not understood, had managed to get her into a School which was a Seminary for Young Ladies.

Before that she had a Governess and her mother also had taught her.

When she was fourteen, after a great deal of talk in which she did not join, she was finaly told she was to be a pupil at one of the most expensive Schools in London.

But, and this was most important, it was not to be known that she was the daughter of Keegan Kenway.

"But why not, Mama?" Isla had asked.

At first her mother had not answered the question, then she said:

"You know, dearest, what a success Papa is on the stage, and it would be very embarrassing if the girls were always talking about him, and perhaps asking you for his autograph."

"Yes . . . I suppose it would be a little . . . uncomfortable," Isla agreed.

"What is more," her mother said, "I have a feeling that the Head Mistress, who is very impressed by the aristocracy, would think that the daughter of an actor should not associate with those who are born into a different way of life."

"Do you mean she disapproved of actors, Mama?"

"Yes, I mean exactly that," her mother had answered.

"Then perhaps it would be a mistake for me to go to that School and be among . . . people who . . . look down on . . . Papa."

Isla knew as soon as she spoke that she had said the wrong thing.

There was a hard note in her mother's voice when she replied:

"You will do what I want you to do! You have to be properly educated, and one day you will thank me."

She paused before she added:

"And who knows—you might one day have to earn your own living."

"How could I do that, Mama?"

"I have no idea," her mother replied, "but if Papa cannot leave you any money, and if you do not get married, at least you will have some means of supporting yourself."

There was almost a note of despair in her mother's voice, and Isla said quickly:

"Of course I will do anything you want, Mama, but it does seem . . . strange."

"I have told the Head Mistress that your name is Isla Arkray, and that you come from Scotland. Arkray, like Isla, is a Scottish name!"

"I hope I shall remember it!" Isla said.

"It was, in fact, the name of your grandmother."

"Is my grandmother still alive?"

"No, dearest, she has been dead a long time; so have my other relatives."

Her mother had turned away as if she did not want to talk about it anymore.

It was only when she was older than Isla thought it strange that her mother seldom if ever talked about her childhood, and never of her father and mother.

All she knew was that she had lived in Scotland, and that seemed very far away.

She had, therefore, gone to School as "Isla Arkray," and because she was very intelligent had moved quickly into a class where the girls were older than she was.

As a newcomer she never had a chance of talking very much.

After her mother died she left School, and it seemed extraordinary that she had been there so long without anyone suspecting that she was Keegan Kenway's daughter.

Very occasionally he would bring the Manager of the

14

Theatre or a very distinguished actor back home.

They would tell Isla how clever her father was, and how much they admired him.

Yet she had the impression that her mother did not welcome people from the Theatre coming to the house.

When she went out with her husband to parties and Isla saw her mother dressed for the evening, she thought that there could be nobody as beautiful as she was.

That was exactly what her father thought too.

"Wherever I take your mother, she is always 'The Belle of the Ball'!" he would say. "And my friends tell me I am the luckiest man in the world, which, of course, I am!"

"And you are so handsome, Papa, I expect that the Ladies think Mama is very lucky too!"

Her father had laughed, and she had known the compliment pleased him.

When she had been in the hall to see them step into the hansom-cab which was waiting for them outside, she thought it impossible that any two people could look so beautiful.

She was aware that none of the fathers of the girls at School could rival her own.

They would usually arrive in smart carriages driven by a coachman in uniform with a cockade in his top-hat and a footman sitting beside him.

Their mothers would wear large crinolines and smart bonnets which were very elegant.

But when Isla compared their faces with her mother's, she knew that no money or title could make one of the Ladies as beautiful as "Mrs. Arkray."

She and her mother would walk away from the School and take a horse-drawn bus, which would carry them as near as possible to their little house.

It was tucked away in a narrow road not far from the Chelsea Hospital.

Isla thought it very romantic because the Hospital had been founded by Nell Gwynne in the days of Charles II.

She was quite sure that if King Charles were still on the throne, he would find her father entertaining, and perhaps they would all be asked to Court at the Palace of Westminster.

However, she had been told that Queen Victoria, although she patronised the Legitimate Theatre, disapproved of the Music Hall.

One thing was quite certain: neither she nor her mother would ever be invited to Buckingham Palace.

However, there were compensations, such as when her mother took her to the Crystal Palace, the Zoo at Regent's Park, and what she enjoyed most of all, the British Museum.

It was then she realised how very well educated her mother was, for she knew a great deal about almost every exhibit.

"Where did you go to School, Mama?"

"In Edinburgh."

"In Scotland?"

"It was a very good School and taught me a great deal. And Edinburgh was a very enjoyable city to live in when I grew older."

Her eyes seemed to be looking back to the past as she said:

"There were lots of Balls and, before I was old enough for them, there were parties for young people."

Isla had been entranced, but when she wanted to question her mother further, she could elicit no more information.

She gradually learnt that her mother had no wish to talk of her childhood, but only of her husband.

He was certainly an exciting person to talk about.

When Isla was old enough, she accompanied him on the piano when he practised the songs he sang.

She found the way he sang fascinating.

He could turn himself from a "la-di-da" smart young man-about-town into a Cockney, selling his wares in the market while he extolled them in song.

What she liked best, however, was when he sang the classical ballads, for which she knew he would be dressed in the armour of a Knight, or as some Shakesperean character.

It was after he joined the Oxford Music Hall that he was identified as a "Heavy Swell," and became the outstanding figure whom all London recognised.

Only when her mother died was Isla aware of the very large part she had played in pushing him to the top.

She would make him practise a ballad over and over again.

She would criticise his movements, his gestures, the inflections of every word he sang.

It was only when her mother was no longer there that Isla realised he would never have been the success he was without her.

Lying in her small bed in the room not far from where her father was sleeping, Isla prayed to her mother for help.

"What am I to do about Papa, Mama?" she asked. "He must have the Benefit, and anyway, it will depress and upset him if he cannot appear when so many people go to the Music Hall just to see him."

As she prayed, she remembered what her father had suggested just before he fell asleep.

She had thought it was an absurd idea.

If it was possible, she wanted to help him, but if that involved her going on the stage, she was sure it was something he would never allow her to do.

She knew what her mother had felt about her going to the Thèatre.

"Why can I not see Papa?" she had asked.

"Because I do not wish you to be known as 'Keegan Kenway's daughter,'" her mother answered.

"But I am proud to be Papa's daughter!"

"I want you to be proud to be yourself," her mother had argued. "You are very lovely, my dearest, and you have a very good brain. You have to learn to stand on your own feet."

"I still cannot understand why that prevents me from watching Papa perform! We could sit in the 'Pit,' and no one would realise we were there!"

Her mother's lips had tightened and she knew that had been the wrong thing to say.

"Please, Mama, let me go just once and watch Papa do that song we were rehearsing yesterday. It has a beautiful tune, and he sings it magnificently."

"I have said 'No,' and I will not discuss it any further!" her mother replied.

Because she knew she had denied Isla something she really wanted, she had taken her instead to the National Gallery.

They had walked round looking at the pictures, admiring and discussing each one.

Her mother had been able to tell her stories of the artists and also to point out the different ways, methods, and styles in which they painted.

It had been delightful, and Isla loved being with her mother.

At the same time, she still longed, if only once, to go to the Music Hall.

"Supposing I do help Papa by taking the place of the lady in the picture," Isla said to herself in the darkness, "it would not be difficult. I can Waltz very well. My dancing-master commended me the last term before I left School."

She thought she could wear one of her mother's gowns, which were very much more elaborate than anything she possessed.

There had been a great banquet the year before her mother died given for all the leading actors and actresses of the London Theatres in which, to his delight, her father had been included.

Her mother had worn a large crinoline of very soft blue silk, ornamented with tiny bunches of musk roses.

The wide bertha was of lace embroidered with pearls and *diamantés* like drops of dew.

"You look exactly like a Fairy Princess, Mama!" Isla had said as her mother kissed her good night. "I wish I were coming with you!"

"I wish you were too," her father had said, "but it is easier for a camel to go through the eye of a needle than to squeeze any more people round the banqueting-table to-night!"

Isla had laughed.

"That is because the Ladies' crinolines take up so much room!" she said.

"I agree with you," her father replied. "At the same time, it makes it more difficult for the gentlemen to dance too close to your mother, which otherwise would make me very jealous and is something I will not allow!"

Her mother smiled.

"The only person I want to dance with is you, darling," she said, "and if anybody is going to be jealous, it is me!"

Her father kissed her.

"You are not only the most beautiful woman in the world," he said, "but to me you are perfection, and everything that a man could ask of a woman."

He had kissed her again before he said:

"The truth is—I love you!"

Isla had seen the happiness in her mother's eyes and told herself that was what she wanted when she married.

They drove away and she went back into the house, shutting the door.

She knew that many people lived in great houses and had very expensive carriages.

But wherever her father and mother went there was love.

That was more important than anything else.

She had, however, felt lonely as she went up to bed.

'Perhaps no one will ever love me,' she thought sadly.

Then she remembered that she resembled her mother.

It was what her father had said often, and also the occasional men from the Theatre who had come to the house.

"It is not fair, Keegan," one of them had remembered, "that you should have a whole Theatre of women applauding you when you are on the stage, and two such beautiful ones waiting for you when you come home."

"I am very grateful for their attention," her father replied, "and you can understand now why I come home as soon as the Show is over."

That had been true when her mother was alive.

Now, Isla thought sadly, she was not important enough in her father's life to prevent him from staying out night after night, drinking too much.

Although she hardly dared express it to herself, she knew he was not looking as handsome as he had been in the past.

"I must help him! I must!" she said aloud.

She had the uncomfortable feeling that if he could not take part in the Benefit tomorrow night, he would drink even more heavily than usual to assuage his disappointment.

"Surely there is somebody who can help him?" she asked, thinking how little she knew of the Theatre.

Once again she was thinking of the strange thing he had said when he told her she could take Letty's place.

"I could do it! I know I could do it!" Isla whispered.

She had an impulse to go into his bedroom and talk it over with her father.

Then she knew he would be fast asleep by now.

It would be sleep induced by the large amount of liquor he had consumed, which would result in him waking up in the morning with a dry mouth and an aching head.

She felt as if everything were too difficult for her to cope with and, like a child frightened in the dark, she cried out for her mother.

"Help me . . . Mama . . . oh . . . please . . . please help us! Everything has gone wrong without you . . . and I am afraid for Papa . . . and if he goes on . . . like this what will . . . happen to . . . both of . . . us?"

Her voice seemed somehow to be lost in the darkness, and she thought her mother did not hear her.

Then it was almost as if her mother were in the room, talking to her as she had when she was small and had woken up crying because of a bad dream.

"It will be all right, darling," she could hear her mother saying. "Quite all right in the end."

chapter two

ISLA stayed awake most of the night worrying over her
father and especially the Benefit.

By the morning, when she had slept for a short while,
she had decided the only thing that could be done was for
her to take Letty Liston's place.

There was no sign of her father at breakfast time.

It was only when luncheon was cooking and waiting on
the stove for his appearance that he came downstairs.

As usual, despite the state he had been in the night before, he looked extremely smart, and to Isla very handsome.

He walked up to her, put his arms round her, and, kissing her cheek, said:

"Forgive me, my dearest, I know I behaved badly last
night."

Isla walked into the Dining-Room, where she had prepared a dish for him to start with which he had always said was one of his favourites.

There was also cold beef left from the steak she had cooked the night before, part of which she had prudently kept back for his luncheon today.

He had never cared for puddings, and instead she had bought him some excellent cheese which was ripe and exactly to his liking.

There was no question of his having any wine or whisky, as there was none left in the house.

Instead, she poured him out a glass of cider which an admirer from the country had given him a month ago, and he drank it without comment.

When he sat back in his chair, obviously feeling better than when he had first come downstairs, Isla said:

"I think, Papa . . . we should talk about what is going to happen . . . tonight."

"Nothing is going to happen!" he said briefly.

"You suggested last night that . . . I should take Letty's place."

"If I let that happen, your mother would turn over in her grave. You know she would never allow you to visit a Music Hall!"

"I think Mama would rather you obtained the Benefit than have us both starve to death!"

"There is no question of that!"

"But there is, Papa, as I discovered this morning when I looked through the bills on your desk."

"You had no right to do that!" her father said angrily.

"I am trying to do what Mama would have done had she been here."

Her father was silent.

She saw the pain in his eyes and knew perceptively that

he was thinking that if her mother were alive, they would not be in the mess they were in now.

"The rent is due next week," Isla said, "and I added up the bills which have been awaiting payment for over three months."

There was silence. Then her father said:

"I do not want to know. They will just have to accept that I cannot pay them until I have made some more money."

"In that case, Papa, your Tailor is threatening legal action. In fact, he insists on having something on account."

"God Almighty . . . !" Keegan Kenway began furiously.

Then, as if he remembered to whom he was speaking, he lapsed into silence.

After a long pause Isla said:

"The only thing we can do, Papa, is for me to come with you tonight and take Letty Liston's place. You have described to me so often what happens and I have also read about it in the newspapers, so I am certain it will not be too difficult."

He did not answer, and after a moment she said coaxingly:

"You said when you taught me the Waltz that I was a very good dancer."

"You cannot do it! You cannot go to the Music Hall!" her father said.

His voice, however, was not as positive as it had been before, and Isla thought he was weakening.

"There is no need for me to see anybody else but you," Isla said quietly. "If you get there at the time you usually arrive, you can come out to meet me at the stage-door. I can do my 'turn,' then go home immediately afterwards."

"It is not as easy as that," her father retorted.

She did not speak, and after a moment he went on:

"It would be impossible for me to leave after I have finished my act, which is in the 'Star' position. All the performers go onto the stage at the end of the Show to take a bow, and on Benefit nights Charles Morton, who owns the Oxford, makes a speech."

"Nobody need see me," Isla said quickly. "It is you they are interested in, Papa."

As her father thought this was true, he made no comment, and Isla went on:

"It is very easy to raise objections, but if we do not pay something towards those bills, I am quite certain that once one of your creditors takes you to Court, a great many others will do the same."

"It is wrong! I know it is wrong!" Keegan Kenway groaned.

"It is far more wrong, if you are sued, for the Press to be able to say nasty things about you," Isla retorted.

She knew by the expression in his eyes that he was contemplating how unpleasant it would be.

He had always been sensitive about his reviews in the newspapers, and when the critics praised him, he was as delighted as a child.

Her mother had always cut out of the newspapers everything that was said about him and pasted it into a scrapbook, and when she died, Isla had carried on.

But there were one or two adverse notices she had hidden from her father, although she suspected he had read them.

In most of the cuttings the critics had praised him and said how much the programme of the Oxford Music Hall had been enhanced by the quality of his performance.

At the same time, one of them had written sarcastically: "He is not as light on his feet as he tries to be, and his features are also heavier."

The most severe critic had printed the words of one of his songs accentuating certain words:

Whoever drinks *at my expense, I treat 'em all the same,*
From Dukes and Lords to cabmen down, I make 'em
drink *Champagne.*

There would have been no harm in that if he had not emphasised the word "drink" in each line by having it printed in italics.

'Papa must be more careful,' Isla thought when she read it, and quickly threw it into the waste-paper basket.

But critics or no critics, she knew that tonight a great number of the audience would be looking forward to hearing Keegan Kenway sing "It Was Only a Dream," and the women would have their handkerchiefs ready.

"It is no use arguing, Papa," she said finally, "but what I would like to do, if you will allow me, is not to wear Letty Liston's gown, which would not fit me, but one of Mama's."

There was a pained expression in her father's eyes, but she knew he was thinking whether theatrically it was a wise or unwise thing to do.

Isla's figure, in fact, measured exactly the same as her mother's, and before he could speak, she said:

"Mama had a gown she wore when you took her to a big party and you said at the time no one looked lovelier than she did."

"I remember," her father said.

There was a thickness about his tone which made Isla go on quickly:

"If I wore that—and I am sure there are some flowers amongst Mama's things with which to make a wreath for my hair—all you have to do is tell me exactly how I get up into the frame and down from it onto the stage."

"One of the stage-hands lifts Letty down," her father said as if the words were dragged from him, "but that is something I will do. I will not allow those young men to touch you."

Isla drew in her breath.

She knew by the way he spoke that he had capitulated.

All she had to do now was to make certain that she did not make any mistakes.

She made him come into the Sitting-Room, and having moved aside the chairs, she hummed while he waltzed her round the floor.

She was very light and insubstantial in his arms.

She loved dancing and found as they whirled round in the very small space that even without music it was exciting.

She knew, however, there would be more room when they were on the stage.

As they stopped dancing, her father said as if the words broke from him:

"I cannot do it! I cannot take you to a place which your mother avoided all her life and from which she would shrink in horror where you are concerned!"

"We cannot go through that all again, Papa!" Isla said. "We have to have the Benefit money, and unless the stars drop out of the sky and fall into our pockets, there is no other way of obtaining it!"

"You will speak to nobody, do you understand? Nobody!" her father said.

"I promise I will do just what you tell me to do," Isla replied.

She felt for the moment that satisfied him.

Because he did not wish her to travel to the Theatre

alone, he decided, after a great deal of thought and argument, to take her with him.

"We will go early," he said, "and I will instruct my dresser that nobody, and I mean nobody, shall come into my Dressing-Room."

Isla agreed to everything he said, not really understanding why he was making such a fuss.

When she was dressed and had put on her mother's beautiful gown, she could not help a little thrill at the idea that for the first time in her life she was going to see a Music Hall.

When he did not discuss the Theatre with her as she was sure he would have done with her mother, she had always felt there was a barrier between them.

This worried her, because she loved him, and she wanted no secrets between them and to know that he trusted her.

When finally she was ready, she went down to her father's bedroom.

He was standing in front of the mirror brushing his dark hair.

He was wearing his evening-shirt with its stiff front and cuffs, and there were two large pearl studs in the front of it, one white and one black.

He always wore them, and Isla knew that her mother had found them in a shop that specialised in artificial jewellery for the stage, and thought they added to her father's smart appearance.

His watch-chain was resplendent across the front of his lovat waist-coat, but that too was false.

The gold watch which he had worn for years had been sold after her mother died to pay for the Funeral.

Keegan Kenway turned from the mirror as Isla entered his room, and for the moment he could only stare at her.

Then he said in a choked voice:

"I thought for a moment you were your mother! You are exactly like her in that gown!"

"I am sure Mama will be helping us tonight," Isla said, "and do not forget, Papa, you have to look after me and tell me exactly what I should do, so that I shall make no mistakes."

Keegan Kenway put on his evening-coat, which was cut with slightly exaggerated square shoulders and an accentuated tightness at the waist.

When he was ready, Isla thought it was impossible for any man to look more handsome or attractive.

She could understand why so many women would be waiting to applaud him.

They took a brougham instead of his usual hansom-cab to the Theatre.

Her father had ordered it earlier in the day because there would be more room for her crinoline.

There was silence as they drove along and Isla, feeling not only excited but also a little frightened, slipped her hand into his.

"You must realise, Papa," she said, "that it is very exciting for me to see for the first time where you work and where you are such a success."

"For the first and the last time!" Keegan Kenway said determinedly.

"Of course! But now I shall be able to talk to you about the Oxford without having to imagine what it looks like inside."

"You have seen it on the outside?"

"Of course!" Isla replied. "Mama and I drove past it soon after it opened and saw your name in huge letters outside. We said a little prayer that you would continue to be such a huge success."

She knew her father was smiling as she spoke, because he always enjoyed compliments.

The brougham turned down a narrow side-street and Isla knew they were at the stage-door.

Because they were early, there was not such a crowd as there would be later.

There were always dozens of women of all ages to watch the performers walk across the pavement and in through the unpretentious doorway.

There were, however, perhaps twenty people there; young girls in saucy hats and older women with shawls over their heads.

There were also a number of rough-looking men who Isla thought were hoping to make a penny or two by holding the horses' heads or running messages.

Her father stepped out first, and there was a cry of delight at the sight of him.

"Keegan Kenway! Keegan Kenway!" women were screaming. "That's 'im orl right. 'E looks a reel Toff, don't 'e?"

They were all laughing, and as Keegan Kenway quickly escorted Isla to the stage-door, they were slapping him on the back.

One woman, her face painted with cosmetics and her eyelashes mascaraed, was saying:

"Give us a kiss fer luck, Guv!"

He pushed past her and hurried Isla through the stage-door.

Just inside, Isla saw an elderly man with white hair eyeing them through what seemed to be a box.

"Oh, it's you, Mr. Kenway!" he exclaimed. "You're early!"

"Yes, I know, Joe. Anything for me?"

"Got some letters—looks like bills ter me. And there's some flowers Oi've stuck up in yer room."

"Thank you, Joe."

Keegan Kenway put his hand under Isla's arm and handed her up an iron staircase which she thought looked as if it should have been swept.

Quickly she lifted her skirts so that they should not be made dirty.

She found, when she reached the top of the staircase, that the passage was in the same condition.

There were doors on either side of it, and from some of them came the sound of voices and laughter.

Her father hurried her quickly to the door at the end of the passage.

When he opened it and went into what she knew was his Dressing-Room, she thought it was exactly what she had expected.

There was a long table against one wall, with a mirror in front of it, on which there was a profusion of grease-paint, powders, and creams.

These came as no surprise to Isla, because she had often been with her mother to purchase at the Theatrical Costumiers, in a street off Leicester Square, what make-up her father needed.

Familiar, too, were, as her father had often described them, the telegrams, photographs, and cuttings from the newspapers which had been pasted on the walls.

There were also one or two posters which had been framed, all with her father's name printed in large letters.

She looked at one and read:

KEEGAN KENWAY THE SMARTEST MAN-ABOUT-TOWN singing his famous songs **"CHAMPAGNE CHARLIE"** and **"IT IS BUT A DREAM."**

In small letters beneath it was written:

WITH LETTY LISTON

Isla made no comment, but looking round the Dressing-Room, she saw there were at least a dozen bouquets of flowers, a number of them so fresh that they could only just have arrived.

There was also a couch on which her father could rest if he wished to do so, and one corner of the room was partitioned off by a curtain.

The purpose of this, she knew, was that when her father entertained a guest, he could change.

However, she knew that her father preferred to come to the Theatre already wearing the clothes in which he would perform.

The curtain was therefore pulled back to reveal a hard wooden chair.

It was rather different from the only other chair in the Dressing-Room which was soft and padded.

Keegan Kenway followed the direction of his daughter's eyes and said:

"If anybody should come in and interrupt us, go behind that curtain and stay there until they have gone."

"Yes, I will do that, Papa."

As she spoke so obediently, he smiled at her.

"You are a good girl, Isla," he said, "and I suppose I am a rotten father to you now that your mother is no longer with us."

"You are nothing of the sort, Papa!" she contradicted. "You are always very kind and very sweet to me. At the same time, you are rather too kind and generous to other people!"

She thought her father looked embarrassed, and she went on:

"Promise me, Papa, that as soon as you receive the Benefit, you will give it to me, and not spend any of it on anybody else."

Keegan Kenway threw out his arms in an extravagant gesture.

"It shall be yours—all yours! I swear it!"

Because she believed him, Isla lifted her face and kissed his cheeks.

"Now what we have to do," he said briskly, "is to ask Nelly to come and put a little bit of paint and powder on your face. You will not need much, but you would look strange without it."

Isla did not answer.

She sat down on the stool in front of the mirror as her father went to the door, opened it, and shouted:

"Nelly! Nelly!"

She could hear his voice echoing down the passage, and after the third time he had shouted, a voice came back:

"All right, all right! I'm a-comin'! I've only one pair o' 'ands!"

A few seconds later a woman came into the Dressing-Room, saying:

"What's 'appened, Mr. Kenway? Don't tell me ye can't apply yer rouge after all these years!"

"No, I can look after myself, Nelly," Keegan Kenway replied, "but I have brought a substitute for Letty, and she needs your help."

The woman, who was middle-aged, stared at Isla and exclaimed:

"God bless me soul! Who's this?"

"I have just told you—she is the replacement for Letty," Keegan Kenway replied.

"Then bust me stays if 'er ain't the prettiest thin' I've seen in years!"

Because the way she spoke was so funny, Isla laughed.

Nelly walked up to her to ask:

"Where've yer bin hidin' so that 'Is Hibs' bring yer 'ere all of a sudden like a rabbit out of an 'at?"

"She is my daughter, Nelly," Keegan Kenway replied. "She has never been in the Music Hall before, and I would not have allowed her to come tonight if it were not for the Benefit."

"I understands yer can't miss that!" Nelly agreed. "The Management was a-wonderin' what yer was goin' to do. . . ."

"And everyone was hoping I would not be able to go on, which would mean more in the kitty for them!" Keegan Kenway remarked.

"Well, they'll 'ave a surprise, won't they?" Nelly asked.

As she spoke, she was looking closely at Isla's face, and finally she said:

"It'd be a mistake to over-paint th' lily. She's that pretty, nobody'll think she's real!"

"I am not only real," Isla laughed, "but also rather frightened."

"Oh, yer'll be all right!" Nelly replied. "One look at yer, an' they'll be certain as Mr. Kenway's up to 'is tricks again!"

She gave a provocative glance at Keegan Kenway as she spoke, and he said quickly:

"Now, come on, Nelly, do the necessary, and do not upset the child."

"I'll not be upsetting 'er," Nelly retorted, "but ye'd better keep 'er under lock an' key or somebody'll be stealin' 'er from yer!"

Isla saw her father frown, and, making no reply, he walked across the room to lock the door.

Nelly picked up the rouge and the hare's foot with which to apply it.

She just touched Isla's cheeks very lightly with it, then powdered her nose, her forehead, and her chin.

Finally, with difficulty, a little mascara was found, because Keegan Kenway did not use it.

Nelly touched the tips of Isla's long eye-lashes, which made her eyes seem larger than they were already.

"I'm not usin' any eye-shadow on anythin' as pretty as this," Nelly said to Keegan Kenway as if he had criticised what she was doing.

She stood back for a moment to see the results of her handiwork, then she said:

"That's enough! She'll look like a dream all right, an' there'll be plenty o' people to tell yer so when the Show's over!"

"Thank you, thank you very much," Isla said politely.

"Now yer be a good girl and go 'ome when yer've done yer bit," Nelly chided. "Ye won't stand a chance if th' gentlemen sees yer, as yer father well knows."

She did not wait for a reply but unlocked the door and went out, pulling it to sharply behind her.

Isla laughed.

"She is very funny!"

"She is also talking sense," Keegan Kenway said.

He walked across the room to open a cupboard, and as

the door of it opened, Isla saw a large bottle of brandy.

"Oh, no, Papa!" she exclaimed.

"I have to have a drink!" her father answered. "I am as nervous as a kitten that something will go wrong."

He poured out what seemed to Isla to be an enormous amount of brandy into a tumbler and added just a splash of soda from the syphon which stood on the dressing-table.

Then with a gesture he directed her to get up from the stool on which she was sitting and took her place.

She sat down in the comfortable padded armchair and watched him as he powdered away the lines under his eyes.

He darkened the skin under his chin, and with a deft touch here and there made himself look ten years younger.

Isla clapped her hands.

"It is so clever the way you do it, Papa."

"I have had enough practise!" he answered. "But, like you, I did not need it when I was younger."

"You must have been very, very handsome when Mama fell in love with you!"

For a moment her father smiled. Then he said quickly:

"You understand exactly what you have to do?"

She knew as he spoke that he did not want to talk about his youth or when he had first loved her mother.

It was something about which they had both been reticent.

Isla had always thought there must have been a great deal of opposition from their families.

Perhaps when they finally married it was without parental approval, and that had meant they were more or less ostracised and on their own.

She remembered the time she had said to her mother:

"Tell me about your childhood, Mama, and when you grew older and met Papa."

Her mother had sometimes been beguiled into telling her how happy she had been when she had been very young, how she had believed there were fairies hidden in the trees and elves burrowing underneath the ground.

The conversation always ended in her reading Isla one of the books which she had loved when she had first been able to read.

"I had such a job finding this one," she said once inadvertently.

"I thought you had brought it with you from your home," Isla said.

Her mother had not answered.

When she was older, Isla thought that, although her mother would not say so, she and her father had eloped together!

Keegan Kenway finished making up, and as he did so there was the noise of voices outside in the passage.

More quickly than he normally moved, he reached the door and turned the key just as somebody knocked on it loudly.

Then a man's voice asked:

"Are you there, Kenway?"

Without being told, Isla moved towards the chair behind the curtain.

When she sat down her father drew the curtain, making certain it was closed at both ends.

Then he walked towards the door and opened it.

"I thought you must be either dead or drunk!" a man's voice said jokingly.

"Good-evening, My Lord! Nice to see you!"

"I am going to ask you and Letty to have supper with me after the Show."

"I am afraid that is impossible!"

"Why?"

The monosyllable was crisp and rather aggressive, Isla thought.

"Letty was taken ill last night," she heard her father explain. "The Doctor sent her to Hospital."

"Good Lord! I have no idea of that! What are you going to do about your turn?"

"I have a substitute, but I have to take her home directly after the Show."

"Nonsense! Nonsense! That would be a waste of time and of her! Meet me at the Café Royale—private room, of course. We will have an amusing supper there."

"That is very kind of you, My Lord, but . . ."

"There are no 'buts' when I am concerned, my boy, and, by the way, I did not think flowers are very appropriate for a man, so I have a case of brandy for you in my carriage."

"Thank you, that is most generous of you," Keegan Kenway said.

"You can thank me by coming to the Café Royale as soon as you can get away from your admirers. We will certainly 'paint the Town red,' tonight!"

Without being able to see him, Isla had the impression that the gentleman who was talking to her father dug him in the ribs.

Then, laughing at his own joke, he left the Dressing-Room and went down the passage.

Keegan Kenway locked the door behind him.

As he drew back the curtain, Isla rose to her feet and said:

"We will not be going to the party, will we, Papa?"

"*You* will not," her father agreed. "I will take you home and join them later."

"Oh, no, Papa!" Isla said involuntarily.

"I have to," her father said roughly, "and Polegate is generous in his own way."

Isla thought of the case of brandy and sighed.

She had thought as she listened to Lord Polegate that his voice sounded thick, rather as if he had already been drinking.

She thought, however, that it would be a mistake to argue with her father.

If he wanted to go to the party, then why should she stop him?

The only thing on which she was determined was that when she went home he would leave the money from the Benefit with her.

There was a knock on the door, and they both started.

"Five minutes, Mr. Kenway!" the call-boy's voice shouted.

"That means when the curtain goes up, does it not, Papa?" Isla asked.

"That is right," her father agreed. "But there is no hurry. We have nearly an hour before we go on."

"I wish I could see the stage."

"You will see all you want to," her father replied.

He spoke reassuringly. At the same time, he picked up the glass of brandy and drank it all.

There was another knock on the door, and once again Isla hurried behind the curtain.

Now as her father answered the door she knew it was a very different kind of caller.

"Why're you locking yourself in, Keegan?" a woman asked.

Her voice was somehow caressing. At the same time, Isla thought she was not very well educated.

"I am busy, Mimi," her father answered. "I have some work to do."

"Work—be damned! You're drinking, that's what you're up to!"

At the expletive Isla started. She had never expected to hear a woman swear.

Then she knew that this caller was the type of person neither her father nor her mother wanted her to meet.

"I am sorry, Mimi, but I really am busy," she heard her father say. "Run along like a good girl, and I expect I will see you later at Polegate's supper party."

"You bet your life you will! And if you flirt with that fair-haired bitch, I'll scratch her eyes out, and make no mistake about it!"

"You behave yourself," Keegan Kenway said, "or you will not be asked again! Polegate is very particular about whom he invites."

"If he asks you, he asks me!" Mimi answered. "And you'd better make it clear to him, or I shall!"

"You go and make yourself look beautiful," Keegan Kenway said. "You will be on soon. It would be a pity if His Lordship did not think you were smart enough to grace his table."

Mimi gave a little scream. Then she said:

"All right, ducks! You win! See you later!"

Once again Keegan Kenway locked the door, then as he pulled apart the curtain he said as if he had to vent his anger on somebody:

"I said you should not come here! It was a mistake, and the sooner you go back home the better!"

"I understand, Papa. At the same time, I wish I could have seen the lady you called Mimi. Is she very pretty?"

"A great many people think so," her father replied reluctantly.

There was silence. Then he said in one of his changes of mood:

"Listen, my precious, you are old enough to understand that whatever you hear or see tonight, you are to forget all about it."

"Of course, Papa."

"Your mother made a home for you and me," Keegan Kenway went on as if he were thinking it out for himself. "We had a little Paradise of our own. The sort of people you have just heard would spoil it, and because it is small they would despise it."

"I know what you are saying, Papa. To us, big or small it is very precious and a house filled with love."

"That is what your mother said."

"And that is what it has always been to me," Isla murmured.

She would have kissed him, then remembered he had grease-paint on his cheeks.

"Just think of tonight as an adventure," he said, "which will never happen again."

There was a worried note in his voice, which made Isla answer:

"Of course, Papa, and do not worry about me. I understand these people are different from anybody I have met before. But I have read about them and, like people in books, they are interesting to study, if not actually real."

Her father laughed.

"You are a good girl, Isla. That is just the right way to think of them."

They sat talking, and although Nelly came back to see if Isla's face was still all right, there were no more interruptions.

Instead, when the door opened, Isla could hear the music and great bursts of applause, and she could see some of what was going on.

At last, after what seemed a long time, her father said they should go down.

He had hardly said the words before there was a knock on the door and the call-boy shouted:

"Three minutes, Mr. Kenway!"

Taking Isla by the hand, he helped her down the dirty stairs.

Then he took her to the side of the stage from where she could see two performers giving a gymnastic display amid roars of applause from the audience.

She caught a glimpse of men turning somersaults, spinning from one man's shoulders to another.

Then she saw there were five men, making a pattern while the central figure stood on his head, his feet spread out.

As the curtain fell, he sprang down onto the stage while the audience applauded enthusiastically and they all made their bows.

Then her father hurried Isla across the stage behind another curtain, at the back of which there was a flight of wooden steps.

He helped her up them into a huge gilded frame.

It was only about five feet from the floor, but Isla felt, as she seated herself on a small stool, that she was very high up.

The stage seemed a long way below her.

The curtain which hid her was of thin, transparent material so that she could see through it, although she knew the audience would not be able to see her.

She clasped her hands in her lap and waited.

The heavy curtains were drawn back and the Chairman, in flowing language, announced her father.

Keegan Kenway came onto the stage, his top-hat at an angle, twirling his cane.

The Orchestra was playing the opening bars of "Champagne Charlie," and as the welcoming applause died away, he started to sing.

His voice had a lilt in it that was irresistible, and because the audience all knew and loved the tune, the whole Theatre seemed to vibrate.

He made it sound much more exciting and sensational than it really was, and soon everyone seemed to be humming and whistling with him.

When he had finished, the whole Theatre seemed to erupt in applause.

Knowing she could not be seen, Isla was able to get a vague view of the vast Auditorium in which there were tables at which people were sitting and drinking.

It seemed to her enormous, and she remembered her father saying that 1,800 people could be accommodated with ease.

Those who did not want to eat or drink were in the Galleries, which she could see were packed.

It was lit, she knew, by four large chandeliers suspended from the central roof, with smaller ones over the Galleries.

What she was trying to calculate was, if the Theatre was full, how much the Benefit would be.

Admission was sixpence, Balcony and Stalls one shilling, private boxes ten shillings sixpence.

"Please God, let it be full tonight!" Isla prayed.

Then as her father came forward to the centre of the stage she kept very still, aware that in a second the thin curtain which hid her would be drawn to one side to reveal the frame.

Some of the people in the Theatre had seen the Show before, and anyway, the rest knew what to expect, so there was a round of applause as soon as the picture became visible to the audience.

Her father was still whistling "Champagne Charlie," and taking a few steps a little unsteadily.

He was an experienced actor, and Isla hoped he was only acting.

She had, however, a suspicion that the brandy he had been drinking continually in his Dressing-Room contributed to making it more life-like than it might have been otherwise.

Then as he sighed and hesitated as if not certain whether he would continue on his way home, he saw the picture just above him and stood still, as if transfixed.

As the audience clapped, Isla had felt a little glow of satisfaction that she had pleased them.

She felt she could understand in a small way how exciting the Theatre could be to those who played in it.

Now the Orchestra began to play a Waltz, and her father in his deep voice said as he looked up at the picture:

"If only you could dance with me! If only I could forget everything but the enchantment of holding you in my arms, how happy it would make me!"

Then, very softly, he began to sing almost as if he were talking to himself:

"Dance with me! Dance with me under the stars,
Dance with me in those magical hours
When you are close in my arms . . ."

He sang so beguilingly that Isla thought any woman who refused him would need to have a heart of stone.

Then, as his voice was silent, the heavy curtains closed and she heard her father say below her:

"Quickly! You are quite safe!"

She moved towards him and he lifted her down, the music swelled, and as they began to dance, the curtains opened.

The applause drowned the sound of the Orchestra as her father waltzed her round and round.

She thought that dancing with him was the most delightful thing she had ever done.

She really felt as if she had wings on her feet, and he, too, was dancing better than she had ever known him to when they had waltzed together in the small Sitting-Room at home.

They went round and round the stage until, as they stopped in the centre, he looked down at her face and she looked up at him.

For a moment they were both absolutely still.

Then he pulled her closer to him, and as she lifted her lips as he had told her to do, the curtain closed once more.

Quickly she ran behind to the steps behind the frame, where stage-hands helped her up.

The curtains opened and a little breathless, but sitting exactly as she had before, Isla was back as a picture.

It was then that Keegan Kenway stood for some seconds with his back to the audience, until with a helpless gesture he walked to the front of the stage and started to sing:

"It Was Only a Dream!"

He did it so skilfully, putting, Isla thought as she listened, more feeling into the words than she had heard him use before, that she almost felt like crying herself.

She knew as he sang that her father was thinking of her mother.

There was no doubt that tonight his voice was clearer than it had been for a long time.

He put all the pathos, all the haunting despair, into the last few lines as he sang only a little above a whisper:

"It Was Only a Dream!"

Isla was certain there was not a dry eye in the Theatre.

The curtain closed and the applause rang out almost deafeningly.

Her father lifted her down from the frame, and going hand in hand in front of the curtain together, he bowed and she curtsied.

Then he took a call alone, and there were whistles and shouts from the hall.

"We want the Dream! Bring on the Dream!"

Listening, Isla thought her father would refuse.

Then a man who she thought must be Charles Morton said as he came back from between the curtains:

"Take her on again—you have to!"

He spoke sharply and it was an order, and once again Keegan Kenway took Isla by the hand.

There was no doubt, as the roar of applause swelled, that that was what the audience wanted.

She curtsied, smiled at them, and curtsied again.

They disappeared behind the curtain, but the applause continued and Charles Morton said:

"Start again with the Waltz!"

"An encore?" Keegan Kenway enquired.

"You are a success, my boy," Charles Morton smiled, "and your partner was an inspiration!"

Keegan Kenway hesitated and Mr. Morton said:

"All right, I'll increase your Benefit. I know that's what you want, but get on with it!"

The Orchestra was playing the music of the dance, and

as the curtains drew back, they were waltzing round and round the stage until they closed again.

Isla ran to the steps and back into the frame, and her father started to sing:

"It Was Only a Dream!"

It was then that Isla suddenly and unexpectedly felt that, although she had been a success, it was a mistake for her to be in the Music Hall.

chapter three

THE curtain-calls at the end of the Show were ecstatic.

A large number of the lady performers received bouquets, and there were even a few for Keegan Kenway.

There was also one for Isla, which she knew had been intended for Letty, but which she accepted gracefully.

Charles Morton announced the Benefit, which amounted to quite a considerable sum, and the performers as they left were each handed their share in a packet.

Isla saw with delight that her father's was quite large.

As they walked off the stage they were surrounded by a number of people, some performers, some members of the audience, all congratulating him and asking who she was.

Isla felt her father stiffen, and after being almost brusque to some of them, he hurried her out through the stage-door.

Outside, there was a huge crowd of admirers cheering and shouting and waving their hats when he appeared.

Isla and her father walked down the narrow street to find their brougham, and Isla was patted on the shoulder or on her arm as the crowd wished her good luck.

It all happened very quickly, and by the time they drove away and her father sat back with a sigh of relief in the carriage, Isla could hardly believe it was true.

She had been on the stage, she had waltzed with her father, she had received some of the rapturous applause which she knew now always greeted him.

Only as the horses moved slowly through the traffic in Oxford Street did her father say:

"This must never happen again!"

"Oh, why, Papa? We were a great success!"

"Your mother would be horrified!"

"I think Mama would . . . understand," Isla said softly, "but . . . please, Papa . . . give me your Benefit."

He had thrust it into his pocket, and she had not missed hearing the number of people outside the Theatre who had said:

"Well done, Kenway! Come to have a drink to celebrate!"

She felt certain that if her father had accepted, as he would normally have done, he would have listened to half-a-dozen "hard luck" stories and practically all the Benefit would have disappeared.

Now she held out her hand and she thought it was with reluctance that he drew it from his pocket and gave it to her.

"You had better let me have a few pounds to spend for the rest of the evening," he said.

"No, Papa!" Isla answered. "I love you, and I think you

are marvellous, but we are deeply in debt and not even the Benefit will pay off all our bills."

There was silence, then her father said:

"I can hardly go to Lord Polegate's party empty-handed."

"Then let him pay for you," Isla said. "He wants you there because you are a success, and because he knows you will make everybody laugh and feel happy. He should be prepared to pay for that!"

Her father gave an exasperated grunt, then he laughed.

"I never expected to be nagged by my daughter," he said. "A mother, yes, or a wife, yes, but not one's small offspring!"

"'Needs must when the Devil drives!'" Isla replied. "The Devil, as far as we are concerned, is the Fishmonger, the Butcher, and your Tailor. There is Bessy, too, who has not been paid for three weeks."

She paused before she went on:

"And there are a whole lot of other bills which will soon grow into big ones!"

She saw her father shrug his shoulders before he said good-humouredly:

"Very well, have it your own way! But if I have to walk home, I shall certainly be very disagreeable tomorrow."

"I am sure Lord Polegate will give you a lift," Isla replied.

The horses drew up outside their small house, and as her father unlocked the door, Isla said:

"I wish you would stay at home with me, Papa, and not go to this party."

"That would be exceedingly rude," her father answered. "Besides, I feel like celebrating the success we have both had tonight."

He helped her from the carriage, and when they reached

51

the small hall, he put his arms around her and said:

"It was very good of you, dearest, but I know it was something you should not have done, and your mother would not have approved."

"I think Mama would feel that we should pay what we owe."

There was a silence, and she had a feeling that her father was once again going to ask her for the Benefit money.

She therefore kissed him quickly and said:

"Go to your party, Papa, but try not to be very late. And as tomorrow is Saturday, do not forget you have an afternoon performance."

"Oh, my God! So I have!" Keegan Kenway said as if it had just come to his mind. "You are right—I will not be late."

He went out through the front-door, shutting it behind him.

*　　*　　*

In the silent house Isla was wishing that she could have gone with him.

She had no idea what sort of party Lord Polegate would give, but she felt sure it would be exciting.

There would be a great number of interesting people, besides some delicious things to eat.

Then she remembered there would also be a lot of drinking, and she wished she had cautioned her father once again not to drink too much.

She had, in fact, been horrified at the amount of brandy he had drunk before going on the stage.

She knew that if he drank a great deal at the supper, especially if it was red wine, he would begin to slur his words.

Perhaps, as she had done on several other occasions, she would have to help him upstairs.

She turned the oil-lamp she had left burning in the hall down low and, lighting a candle, carried it upstairs to her bedroom on the second floor.

She took off her mother's gown.

As she did so, she could smell the sweet fragrance of the perfume her mother had always used, and it brought her memory back even more vividly than the gown did.

When she got into bed, Isla prayed that her father would come home early, that he would not drink too much.

If, moreover, she impressed on him that they must not get into debt again, perhaps he would be less generous every week with his salary.

There seemed to be a whole list of things she had to pray about, and it was a long time before she fell asleep.

* * *

Isla awoke with a start, looked at the clock by her bed, and saw with surprise that it was nearly nine o'clock.

She was used to rising at seven.

But she realised that the excitement of the night before and the anxiety she had felt in case she made a mistake had made her very tired.

Now she jumped out of bed and, ten minutes later, was hurrying down the stairs, moving very softly so as not to wake her father.

As she reached the first floor, she saw that the door of his bedroom was ajar, and she wondered whether he had left his clothes on the floor.

Perhaps if he was very late, he had slept in them.

Very gently, holding her breath, she opened the door a few inches so that she could look inside.

Then by the light of the sunshine seeping through the

53

sides of the curtains she saw quite clearly that the bed had not been slept in.

The sheets which she had folded back before they left for the Theatre were exactly as she had left them.

She opened the door as wide as it would go and realised that her father had not come home last night.

It was the first time since her mother's death that he had stayed out all night, even though he had often returned in the small hours of the morning.

Now there was no sign of him, and it gave her a shock.

What could have happened? Why had he stayed away without letting her know?

She would find no answer to her questions as she went slowly down the stairs.

The only thing she could think was that he must have drunk far too much, and his host, Lord Polegate, had no idea where he lived.

He would surely, if he had known, have taken him back to his house.

He would hardly have left him in the Restaurant.

Isla felt helpless and very much alone.

She forced herself to go into the kitchen, light the stove, and start to prepare breakfast, so that when her father did come home he would not have to wait too long for it.

She did not eat anything herself, but poured out a cup of coffee and drank it slowly.

She was expecting every minute to hear the sound of wheels outside the front door and know her father had returned.

It was unfortunately not the morning that Bessy came.

She had been yesterday, and Isla felt that even her constant complaining about her rheumatism would be better than having no one to talk to.

An hour later, when there was still no sign of her father,

she fetched his Benefit money, which she had taken upstairs with her.

Sitting down at the desk in the Sitting-Room, she found the bills which she had put tidily in a drawer and apportioned the money out amongst them.

She could not pay the whole of her father's account with his Tailor.

But she knew that as the Tailor took the largest amount of the Benefit, they would be satisfied for at least a month or two.

She put the money into envelopes and sealed them down.

She decided that as soon as her father returned and was in bed, she would hurry to the Butcher, the Fishmonger, and the Grocer.

She was sure they would be pleased with what she had to give them.

By eleven o'clock she was growing worried and every few minutes went to the window to look out and see if there was a carriage of any sort coming down the narrow road.

But there was only a man with a hurdy-gurdy and a poor, miserable-looking monkey sitting on top of it, and two or three errand-boys whistling "Champagne Charlie."

It made her feel more anxious than she was already.

Then, as she could not bear to go on waiting but felt she must do something, she put on her bonnet and ran to the shops.

She gave the tradesmen the envelopes with the money inside and hardly waited to hear their thanks, in case her father had arrived home while she was out.

The Tailor was in another part of London altogether.

She planned that if her father was taking a carriage to

the Theatre for the afternoon performance, she could go with him.

He could drop her off as near as possible to Savile Row, and when she had given the Tailor the envelope, she would take a horse-drawn bus back to Chelsea.

It all seemed to plan itself out quite easily until when she turned towards home she realised as she looked up the street there was no carriage outside their house.

It was then she began to feel frightened not only because her father was so late, but also because he obviously must have forgotten about the afternoon performance.

"Surely somebody will remind him?" she asked herself.

She let herself into the house, took off her bonnet, and wondered what she should do or where she could turn for help.

It seemed extraordinary that she had no idea who her father's friends were or where they lived.

She went into the kitchen to see if the fire was still burning in the stove, and when she was there she heard a knock on the front-door.

She gave a little cry of delight, thinking it must be her father, and ran across the small hall to fling open the door.

She had a quick impression of a man with a top-hat on his head standing outside, and exclaimed:

"Papa!"

Even as she spoke she realised it was not her father who stood there.

The gentleman facing her was very smartly dressed, and behind him she saw an extremely elegant carriage drawn by two well-bred horses.

There was a coachman on the box and a footman standing by the carriage door.

Then the gentleman said:

"I am not mistaken! And you are even more beautiful in the daytime than you were last night!"

Isla looked at him in surprise, and he said:

"My name is Polegate, Lord Polegate, and I cannot tell you how disappointed I was that you did not come to my party."

Isla drew in her breath to ask what had happened to her father, but before she could speak, Lord Polegate went on:

"May I come in? I have something to tell you."

He took off his hat and entered the house, and she saw him look round the small hall as if he despised it.

She lifted her chin a little higher and, opening the door of the Sitting-Room, said:

"You had better come in, My Lord. Can you tell me what has happened to my father? He went to your party last night, and I have not seen him since."

"That is the reason I have called on you," Lord Polegate replied.

"He is . . . ill?"

The words were a cry.

Lord Polegate moved across the small Sitting-Room and seated himself in an armchair by the window.

He had put his top-hat on a table in the hall and Isla realised his hair was flecked with grey and he appeared to be quite elderly.

At the same time, he had an air of consequence about him which she found rather awe-inspiring.

"I have been very, very . . . worried about Papa," she said quickly. "Please tell me what has . . . happened."

"I suggest you sit down, Miss Kenway," Lord Polegate said, "for I am afraid the news is not at all good."

"Papa . . . is ill?"

"Your father was taken ill," Lord Polegate said slowly,

"very late last night, or perhaps I should say early this morning."

"What . . . happened?"

As she spoke, Isla was quite certain that her father had had too much to drink.

Yet if that was so, by this time he should have recovered and Lord Polegate would have brought him here with him.

"I called the Doctor to your father," His Lordship went on, "and he thinks he has had a slight heart-attack. As he was not capable of telling us where he lived, I took him to my house in Park Lane, and that is where he is at the moment!"

"That was very kind of you," Isla said, "and if he comes home, I can nurse him."

"I assure you, he is being very well looked after and is very comfortable," Lord Polegate replied.

His eyes looked her over in a way she found very embarrassing before he added:

"I am, of course, extremely sorry that your father is unwell. But it has given me a chance to meet you—something I was very eager to do after I had seen you last night."

The way he spoke made Isla feel a little uncomfortable, and she said quickly:

"Would it be possible, My Lord, for me to see Papa immediately? I could then decide whether it would be best for him to come back here."

"I have already told you that I will look after your father," Lord Polegate said, "but I think it would be a good idea that you should come with me to see him."

"Oh, thank you!" Isla said. "Thank you very much."

She got to her feet and only as she reached the door did she think that perhaps she was being rude, and she turned back to say:

"Is there anything I can get Your Lordship? There is some coffee ready, if that is to your liking."

"Thank you, but I have already had breakfast," Lord Polegate said, "and I promise that you and I will enjoy a delicious luncheon together after you have seen your father."

"I will go to get my bonnet," Isla answered.

She dropped him a small curtsy and ran up the stairs.

She was thinking as she did so that she would have to change, and must be as quick as possible.

She had not been able to buy any new clothes for a long time, but before her mother died she had bought her a very pretty gown with a small crinoline that had a velvet coatee to wear over it.

She quickly changed, and put on the bonnet trimmed with blue ribbon that matched her gown.

As she took her gloves from the top drawer of her dressing-table, she saw the envelope for the Tailor that she had put there for safety before she left the house.

It seemed slightly impertinent, but she could not help feeling that Lord Polegate was, in a way, responsible for her father being ill.

She thought, therefore, she could ask him if one of his servants could deliver a letter to the Tailor's.

She hurried down the stairs with it in her hand, and as she entered the Sitting-Room he was still in the armchair where she had left him.

She thought as she walked towards him that he appraised her in a manner that she felt was almost insulting.

Then she told herself she was being imaginative and as one of her father's friends, she was sure he was very kind.

"You have been quick, my dear," he said with a slightly mocking note in his voice.

"I . . . I did not want to keep you waiting . . . My Lord," Isla said.

Slowly Lord Polegate got to his feet.

"Of course you are expecting me to tell you how lovely you look," he said, "far lovelier than anybody I have seen for a very long time."

"Your Lordship is most gracious . . . but I am very . . . anxious to . . . reach my father as . . . speedily as . . . possible."

"Yes, of course," he said, "and is that a present you have for him?"

He was looking at the envelope in her hand, and Isla said:

"I . . . I wondered if we could leave this on our way to your house . . . or if Your Lordship would be . . . kind enough to see that it is . . . delivered . . . later in the . . . day."

She stammered over her words because she felt he was looking at her in a strange manner.

"So your *billet doux*," he said, looking again at the envelope, "is not for some charming young man, but for your father's Tailor."

"It contains money, My Lord, and that is why I have to be . . . careful of it. Perhaps it would be better if I . . . delivered it in person."

"I will see that it is taken safely to its destination," Lord Polegate said. "Shall I guess that it contains money from your father's Benefit to pay an overdue bill?"

He made what he said sound almost as if he were pleased at having solved a difficult conundrum.

Isla, wishing she had left the money in the dressing-table drawer, moved towards the door.

Lord Polegate followed her, and he did not speak until they were in the carriage.

As the horses moved off he said:

"You know I am ready to give you anything you wish for, and, if it is just a question of your father's debts, leave them to me."

What he said was so surprising that Isla turned to look at him, her eyes very wide in her small face.

"Your Lordship is extremely kind," she said after a moment, "but the ... Benefit which my father received last night has for the moment ... swept away our ... worries."

"No one as beautiful as you should have to worry about money," Lord Polegate remarked.

Isla found his compliments embarrassing and turned her head away to look out of the window on her side of the carriage.

"I mean what I say," Lord Polegate said, "and after luncheon you must tell me what you would like most—diamonds? sables? No! I think because you are so young it should be ermine!"

Isla turned to stare at him in sheer astonishment.

It struck her that if he was not drunk, which was unlikely at this hour of the morning, he must be a little mad.

She could not imagine that anyone would talk in such an exaggerated manner if they were not in some way slightly deranged.

Because he was obviously waiting for her answer, she said after a moment:

"All that concerns me at the moment, My Lord, is my father ... and it is difficult to think of ... anything else."

Lord Polegate smiled and, turning a little sideways in his seat, said:

"In which case, I can just look at you. You know how unusual you are, and how different from anyone Kenway has produced in the past."

"Then you cannot have met my mother, My Lord!"

"No, I did not have that pleasure," Lord Polegate said.
"In fact, I have known your father only for the last six
months."

Isla had no reply to this, and they drove on in silence.

She was, however, acutely aware that Lord Polegate
was watching her, and it made her feel uncomfortable.

She was, therefore, greatly relieved when the horses
drew up outside a large porticoed door of what she realised
was one of the large houses in Park Lane.

There was a red carpet on the steps, four footmen in
livery, and a Butler in the hall. As they entered, Lord Polegate said:

"Miss Kenway wishes to see her father, and I want
luncheon in half-an-hour."

"Very good, M'Lord!"

"Come with me," Lord Polegate said to Isla.

They climbed the very impressive staircase side by side,
and walked along the wide corridor at the end of which
Lord Polegate knocked on a door.

It was opened almost immediately by a man dressed as a
valet.

"How is our patient, Hales?" Lord Polegate asked.

"'E's never stirred, M'Lord, an' the Doctor's comin'
again this afternoon."

Lord Polegate walked into the room and Isla followed
him.

Then, as she saw her father's head on the pillow of a
large bed, she ran to his side.

His face was very pale, his eyes were closed, and for a
moment a streak of fear like the thrust of a dagger went
through her, as she thought he was dead.

Then, as she bent forward to touch his hand, she realised it was warm and he was definitely breathing.

Despite his pallor he looked very handsome, and because she could not help herself, she bent nearer to him to say in a low voice:

"Papa! Papa! Can you hear me?"

There was no response, and the hand under hers was quite still.

She looked at him, feeling frightened and helpless.

Then she was aware that Lord Polegate and the valet were standing and waiting as if for her to say something.

"W-what . . . can we do?" she asked in a whisper.

"There is nothing we can do, my dear, that has not been done already," Lord Polegate replied. "My valet says the Doctor will be coming again this afternoon, and perhaps by then your father will have regained consciousness. In the meantime we shall just have to wait and see."

"But . . . I cannot leave him . . . here!" Isla said.

"Why not?"

"Because I must be with him."

Lord Polegate smiled.

"That is quite easy. My house is large, and there is plenty of room for you."

It never struck her that he would say anything like that, and as she stared at him, he said:

"We will talk it over while we have luncheon. I assure you your father will be very well looked after by Hales."

He walked purposefully towards the door, but Isla turned back.

She bent and kissed her father's cheek very lightly, and there were tears in her eyes as she prayed silently that he would soon be better.

Then, knowing there was nothing else she could do, she followed Lord Polegate out into the corridor, only saying "Thank you" to the valet as she passed him.

They walked in silence down the stairs and into the most luxurious Sitting-Room Isla had ever imagined.

There were pictures on the wall, and she knew, because her mother had taken her to the National Gallery and other Museums, that they were all priceless masterpieces.

The furniture was also superb, and she recognised the carpet on the floor as being an Aubusson.

Lord Polegate had poured her a glass of champagne, and the bottle was reposing in an elaborate gold ice-cooler which bore his crest.

"You will feel better after you have had a drink, my dear," he said. "It is always a shock to see someone one loves unconscious."

"How could . . . this have . . . happened to Papa?" Isla asked. "And why should he have . . . suffered a heart-attack?"

She looked at Lord Polegate almost accusingly as she asked the question, and he said with a meaningful gesture of his hands:

"I am afraid, my dear, your father had imbibed rather too freely, and he had also eaten a great deal for supper."

Isla shut her eyes for a moment.

She could imagine how bad it had been for her father to drink a great deal on top of the brandy he had already consumed.

At the same time, he had always seemed so strong, and she could hardly believe he could collapse in such a frightening manner.

She thought of him lying pale and ill upstairs and felt as if the world were something very dark, and she was afraid.

"Now, you are not to worry yourself," Lord Polegate said in a caressing voice. "I am a great friend of your father's, and I will look after him, and I will also look after *you*."

He seemed to emphasise the last word.

As she glanced at him, then looked away again, she told

herself he might be kind, but he was somebody she did not understand.

To her relief, the Butler announced that luncheon was ready, and they went into a large, impressive and, to Isla, a very beautiful Dining-Room.

The walls were hung with magnificent Pictures, and the chairs were upholstered in crimson velvet.

There seemed everywhere she looked to be gold and silver gleaming in the sunshine coming through the windows.

She was so worried and upset that she thought she was not hungry.

She had, however, been too nervous to eat anything last night before they went to the Theatre and too tired when her father had left her at home afterwards to bother about food.

Today she had made herself no breakfast, so she was, in fact, now very hungry.

If she had not been so upset, she knew she would have enjoyed the delicious dishes which followed one after the other.

She thought she would like to provide them for her father when he was well enough to enjoy them.

Since the Butler and the footmen were in the room throughout the meal, Lord Polegate did not pay her compliments but talked somewhat boastfully of his possessions.

"I would like you to see my horses," he said. "Although I say it myself, my race-horses as well as my carriage-horses are unbeatable!"

He laughed and added:

"Although those who are envious of me try to beat me!"

Isla then asked:

"Where do you keep your horses?"

"My race-horses are at Newmarket, but the horses I ride are at my country estate, which is not far outside London."

He gave a little exclamation.

"I have an idea! I cannot imagine why I did not think of it before!"

"Think of what?" Isla asked, because she felt it was expected of her.

"If the Doctor, when he calls, thinks your father will remain in a coma as he is at the moment, I will drive you down to my house and you can see my horses for yourself!"

"It is very kind of you to think of it," Isla replied, "but I would not want to leave Papa."

"It would not take long," Lord Polegate said, "and until he wakes, what can you do?"

"I wish to be there when he does," Isla said.

"Well, we can easily find out when that will be. My own Specialist, whom I consider to be the best in London, will be here at two o'clock."

He called the Butler and said:

"Order my Chaise and four horses for two-thirty. I am driving down to Polegate. Send a groom ahead immediately to inform them of my intentions."

"Very good, M'Lord."

"No, no!" Isla tried to say, but Lord Polegate did not seem to hear her.

As they left the Dining-Room she told herself she wanted to stay with her father.

He was the only thing that seemed real in a strange new world that had started with her appearance on the stage at the Oxford.

Now it was continuing with her finding it impossible to refuse to drive to the country with this old man.

She was sure it was something her mother would not have allowed her to do.

Yet however much she tried to protest, Lord Polegate did not appear to listen, or did not intend to.

'I have to convince him that I need to be with Papa!' she thought.

He had moved back into the Sitting-Room, which she had heard the Butler refer to as "The Salon."

She was just wondering how she could explain to Lord Polegate that she must stay with her father, when the Butler announced:

"Sir Martin Simpson, M'Lord, has just arrived!"

"I will speak to him at once!" Lord Polegate replied, getting to his feet.

Isla would have risen, too, but he said:

"Stay here, my dear, he will talk to you after he has seen your father."

He went from the room, shutting the door behind him.

Isla started to pray that her father would not be as bad as he appeared to be, and also that she could take him home.

He might be very comfortable in this luxurious house, but she was sure it was a nuisance for Lord Polegate to have a guest who was unconscious and required nursing.

"Please, God, make Papa better . . . please . . . please . . . " she prayed.

The door opened and Lord Polegate returned, smiling.

"Now, you are not to worry your pretty head," he said. "Sir Martin is a very sensible man and without exception the best Doctor in London. He tends Her Majesty, and one could not have a better recommendation."

He laughed before he said:

"Your father will have the best treatment as the King of his profession, a *Lion Comique* who stands head and shoulders above all his imitators."

67

"I am glad you have such a high opinion of Papa," Isla said.

"I would rather tell you my opinion of you," Lord Polegate said. "It will take me a long time, and I shall be very eloquent on the subject."

"N-no . . . please . . ." Isla said.

She walked away from him towards the window, feeling in some manner she could not understand that he was encroaching on her.

She had no idea, with the sunshine on her fair hair and her profile silhouetted against the polished glass, how lovely she looked.

Lord Polegate did not follow her, he merely watched her, and there was a faint smile on his thick lips which would have frightened her had she seen it.

It was not long before Sir Martin Simpson came into the room.

"Ah, here you are, Sir Martin!" Lord Polegate said. "Now let me introduce you. Miss Kenway, this is the best, the most famous, and cleverest Physician in the whole country!"

Sir Martin laughed.

"Now you are making me nervous! I am delighted to make your acquaintance, Miss Kenway, and tell you I am a great admirer of your father's."

"How is he?" Isla asked.

Sir Martin shook his head.

"He is still unconscious, and I am rather afraid that besides having had a heart-attack, he has also suffered a slight stroke."

Isla gave a little cry of horror, and Sir Martin went on:

"It may be nothing at all serious, but he must be kept absolutely quiet. It is best for him to have no visitors for at least forty-eight hours, not even you, my dear lady."

"But . . . I must be . . . with . . . him!"

"I think it would be wiser not, and I understand that your host, my old friend Lord Polegate, has suggested taking you to the country. I think that is an excellent idea!"

"But . . . please . . ." Isla began.

"What you have to do," Sir Martin interrupted, "is to get yourself really fit in order that when your father recovers, you can give him hope and strength so that he will soon be back on the stage. We cannot do without him, you know."

Isla wanted to know more, but Sir Martin had already turned to Lord Polegate.

"Goodbye, My Lord," he was saying. "I will call again tomorrow morning and again in the afternoon. I know my patient is in very good hands. In fact, as I have told you before, Hales is an excellent man and will carry out my instructions."

"Thank you, Sir Martin, and thank you for coming," Lord Polegate said. "I shall take your advice and carry Miss Kenway off to the country to put some roses in her cheeks!"

Almost before Isla could curtsy or thank him for coming, Sir Martin had gone.

Lord Polegate came back into the room, saying:

"Now we really must obey instructions. I am sure you would like to go upstairs and tidy yourself, and the horses will be around in ten minutes."

"I would much rather stay here," Isla protested.

"Against Doctor's orders?" Lord Polegate said in pretended horror. "You know as well as I do that Doctors are like gods whom we have to obey. Now, hurry, my dear, I do not like to be kept waiting."

There was nothing Isla could do but do as she was told.

She went up the stairs and was taken into a beautiful bedroom.

It was not unlike the one her father was occupying, and she was shown into the room by a Housekeeper in rustling black with a chatelaine at her waist.

Isla washed her hands and tidied her hair and felt as if she were being swept along on a tidal wave from which she could not extract herself.

She insisted, however, on going back to her father's room and having one last look at him.

He was lying just as they had left him.

The blinds were half-drawn and the room was dim and cool, and she knew that Lord Polegate was right in saying he was comfortable and well looked after.

"I am being very foolish to complain instead of just being grateful," she told herself.

At the same time, she had the feeling it was a mistake for them both to stay here.

Whatever the Doctor or Lord Polegate said, they would be far better off if they were at home in their own small house, where they had been so happy with her mother.

When she reached the top of the staircase, Lord Polegate was in the hall below.

As he looked up at her, the light coming from the open front-door was on him, and she saw there was a bald patch on the top of his head.

He was indeed, she thought, an old man.

'I suppose it does not matter my being with him unchaperoned,' she thought, 'although Mama might think it very unconventional.'

She told herself that once again she was being ungrateful.

No one could be more kind or considerate than Lord Polegate.

When her father was well enough, she was certain he would be given the same delicious food she had enjoyed at luncheon.

"Very much better than I can give him!" she told herself.

Then, as she reached the bottom of the stairs, Lord Polegate unexpectedly took her hand in his and raised it to his lips.

"Once again you are punctual," he said, "and I think, my lovely young lady, this is an exciting moment when I can show you my country-house, my horses, and many other things which I know you will enjoy."

"You are . . . very kind," Isla said.

She took her hand hastily away from his and put on her gloves.

The Chaise she recognised as being as smart, if not smarter, than anything she had seen in Rotten Row.

It was drawn by four magnificent black horses without a touch of white on them anywhere.

Lord Polegate picked up the reins, the grooms jumped up into the small seat behind them, and they were off.

It would have been impossible for Isla not to enjoy driving in such magnificent style, and she realised that Lord Polegate was an expert driver.

They seemed to move at an extraordinarily quick pace through the traffic and out into the countryside.

She knew they were going North, and she wondered if Lord Polegate's house in the country was as magnificent as the one they had just left.

'He must be very rich,' she thought to herself.

As if what she was thinking communicated itself to him, he asked:

"Are you admiring my horses? They cost me a fortune, but I consider the money well spent."

"They are very . . . fine."

"Do you ride?"

"Whenever I get . . . the chance," Isla replied.

She had ridden, when they could afford it, almost every day, but it had only been in the Park.

She had often longed to be able to ride in the country, where there were no restrictions.

"Now is your opportunity!" Lord Polegate said. "I will mount you tomorrow on one of the finest horses you have ever seen."

"Tomorrow?" Isla questioned.

"We will ride tomorrow morning," he said, "if you are not too tired."

Isla smiled.

"I am afraid that is impossible."

"Why?"

"Because, My Lord, I have no habit at the moment, having grown out of the one I wore in the past."

"I am sure we can find one for you," Lord Polegate said.

She thought he was being ridiculous, but he went on:

"My Housekeeper in the country has a variety of different clothes for almost every occasion. She has collected them over the years from my sisters, my nieces, and a number of careless guests who always seem to leave things behind them."

Isla looked puzzled.

"Tomorrow we shall be in London," she said, thinking Lord Polegate must have forgotten.

"In London?" he said quickly. "Of course not! You are coming to stay with me, my dear, and I cannot tell you how much I am looking forward to being your host, and how thrilled I am to have you as my guest!"

chapter four

WHEN Isla saw Lord Polegate's house she was disappointed.

Because he seemed so rich and his horses were excellent, she had somehow imagined he would be living in one of the huge Georgian mansions which her mother had often described to her.

She had also seen pictures of them in the magazines.

Instead, it was, she thought, quite obviously a house built at the beginning of the century, rather pretentious, with a great many gables and windows.

But it was not symmetrically beautiful, as she had hoped.

She had often read of the houses which were described so vividly in the *Illustrated London News*, or *The Graphic* but which she thought belonged to a world she would never enter.

She knew that some of the girls at School had lived in houses of exactly that sort.

They also talked of the garden-parties their parents gave in the summer, and the house-parties in the winter.

Isla had felt very out of sorts.

She could hardly describe to them the tiny little house in which she lived with her parents.

She was, however, not envious, merely curious.

When Lord Polegate told her he was taking her to the country, it flashed through her mind that now she would be able to see at close quarters the houses about which she had heard so much.

One thing she had learned, both from her mother and at School, was an appreciation of what was architecturally whole and well proportioned.

Lord Polegate's rambling mansion was neither of these things.

She was, of course, too polite to say so, and admired the drive and the gardens, which were bright with colour.

At the same time, she was worrying about whether she was doing something wrong in going to stay with Lord Polegate in the country.

It seemed strange that he had not told her before they left London, so that she could have brought her own things with her.

He had swept her away in such a precipitate manner that she had hardly had time to think.

If she had been given time to pack, she would certainly have considered the invitation in a different light.

But when he talked about the clothes of his sisters and nieces, she told herself she was being very stupid.

Of course some of them would be there, and it would be

pleasant to meet some young people of her own age.

As they drew up at the front-door, there was a red carpet laid down the steps.

Also there seemed an innumerable number of footmen in very smart livery which had a great deal of gold braid on it.

"I am sure you are hungry," Lord Polegate said, "and I know I am. There will be a glass of champagne waiting for you in the Sitting-Room, although first, I am sure, you will want to take off your bonnet."

"That would be nice," Isla agreed.

A footman led the way upstairs to where on the landing was waiting the Housekeeper.

She seemed almost identical to the one she had seen at Lord Polegate's house in London.

She did not seem, however, very welcoming in her attitude as she led Isla along the passage.

Almost at the end of it she opened a door, and they went into what Isla thought was a magnificent room.

It was certainly very large, and it seemed to be crammed with furniture that was all very ornate, inlaid and ornamented, with burnished gold handles.

The bed, which was draped with curtains, was also gilded and betasselled.

The frame of the mirror on the dressing-table was a riot of angels holding up garlands of flowers.

It ought, Isla thought to herself, to have been impressive and very beautiful, and yet it somehow missed it.

The Housekeeper in a frigid voice showed her the wash-hand-stand, on which there was a can of warm water.

She was provided as well with a brush and a comb for her hair.

The Housekeeper looked so disapproving as she waited on her that Isla wondered if she resented Lord Polegate having guests because they gave her extra work.

She was, however, not so troubled about the House-keeper as about herself.

"How can I stay here with not even a nightgown to wear?" she asked herself.

She thought it was really very inconsiderate of Lord Polegate not to have given her time to pack what was necessary.

At the same time, she had the uncomfortable feeling that she should have stayed in London to be near her father.

"If he regains consciousness and I am not there, he will think it strange," she told herself.

She decided she must try to persuade Lord Polegate to take her back to London that afternoon.

When, however, she tried to broach the subject to him downstairs, he replied:

"How can you be so foolish, my dear, as to want to stay alone in your house?"

"But . . . supposing Papa recovers consciousness? I could never forgive myself, knowing that I had left him to face the situation with nobody to turn to."

"You could, of course, have stayed at my house in London," Lord Polegate said as if he had just thought of it, "but as the Doctor assured me there was no chance of your father regaining consciousness before tomorrow, I was sure a little fresh air will do you good."

It all sounded quite plausible, but Isla still felt uncomfortable, especially from the way Lord Polegate looked at her.

When she had come downstairs, worrying as to how she should approach him to take her home, he had taken her hand in his.

Once again, to her surprise, he had kissed it.

"You are entrancing!" he said. "I have never seen anybody quite so lovely, so spring-like, and that is why, my dear, I know this is the right frame for you rather than the one in which you sat last night!"

Isla tried to laugh, but it was rather difficult when he was still holding her hand and his face seemed uncomfortably near to hers.

He, however, released her and persuaded her to drink a little champagne.

"Now we are going to enjoy ourselves," he said. "You are going to be a very brave girl and not worry about your father, who is in the hands of the finest Physician in England. Instead, you must be a little grateful to me because I am looking after you."

"I am very . . . grateful," Isla said.

He made her feel as if she had been rude, and she therefore said quickly:

"If I have not thanked you, it is because I feel a little bewildered at everything happening at once, but I am indeed very, very grateful."

"You can show me how grateful you are later," Lord Polegate said.

She did not know what he meant by this, but then luncheon was announced, and he took her into a large Dining-Room.

They sat at a table which could easily have accommodated twenty or thirty guests and in consequence made Isla feel small and insignificant.

But Lord Polegate was very much at his ease.

The food, which was excellent, was served to them on silver dishes, and they talked about the Theatre and the brilliant success of the Oxford.

"Charles Morton has made a great deal of money out of it," he said. "I expect you know it was originally an old

Posting House dating back to the sixteenth century."

Isla was instantly interested.

"Papa never told me that," she said, "but then, he seldom talks about the Music Hall."

"I expect he wants to keep you away from the stage," Lord Polegate said, "and who shall blame him? You are too pretty to get mixed up with all that froth and glitter!"

"I thought . . . last night," Isla said in a hesitating little voice, "that it was . . . not as . . . glamorous as I had expected."

"That is because you were on the stage, and not in front of it," Lord Polegate replied, "but to those like myself in the audience you looked so beautiful that I could not at first believe you were real."

Isla laughed.

"Did you think I was really a picture?"

"It was one I have always wanted to own," Lord Polegate said. "But if I cannot hang you on the wall, I have done the next best thing in bringing you here."

She thought he was trying to be funny, but the way he spoke seemed serious, and she said quickly:

"It is very kind of you, and I see you have some exceedingly fine pictures in this room and on the stairs."

"They cost a great deal of money," Lord Polegate said, "but I do not suppose you are interested in pictures as much as in jewels."

"Mama and I went to see the Crown Jewels in the Tower of London," Isla said.

"Did you wish you could try on a crown?"

"They looked rather heavy," Isla replied. "Mama said she felt sorry for the Queen when she had to wear one, and for the Ladies who wear tiaras in the evening."

Once again Isla was thinking of the pictures she had seen in magazines.

"I do not think a tiara would suit you," Lord Polegate replied, "but a necklace of pearls would be very appropriate or perhaps you would prefer diamonds."

"As I am unlikely to own either," Isla smiled, "that is something I have not considered."

"Then consider it now," Lord Polegate answered, "because when we return to London, I shall choose you a necklace and bracelets to match the sparkle in your eyes."

Isla stared at him, thinking he was joking.

Then, as she realised he was speaking as if that were what he wanted to do, she said quickly:

"I know you are teasing me, and what I would like to look at is your beautiful garden."

"And I would rather look at you!" Lord Polegate said.

Now there was a note in his voice and an expression on his face that made her feel frightened.

When they finished luncheon there was coffee, and a glass of port was put in front of Lord Polegate.

The servants had now withdrawn, and quite suddenly Isla felt lost.

She was alone in the big room with an elderly man who said such strange things which she did not really understand.

She was sure he was only teasing her, at the same time he seemed serious, and it was difficult to know how to reply to the things he said.

As if he sensed that he was going too quickly, he said:

"What would you like to do? I feel it would be rather hot in the garden, and perhaps you would rather come to the stables and see my horses."

"I would love to do that!" Isla said eagerly.

Lord Polegate looked at the clock.

"I think it is too late to ride today, after we have had such a long drive. We will choose the horses we will ride tomorrow. I am sure Mrs. Blowfeld, the Housekeeper, can find you a habit."

"I think I ought to go back to London tomorrow," Isla said in a small voice. "I would not want Papa to wake up and miss me."

"We will talk about that tomorrow morning," Lord Polegate promised.

As she followed him from the Dining-Room, she had the uncomfortable feeling that it was going to be difficult to get back to London.

How she wished with all her heart that she had insisted on staying there.

She, however, forgot everything but the horses when they reached the stables.

They were certainly a very impressive display of well-bred, perfectly trained horse-flesh.

Whenever Isla had been able to ride in Hyde Park, she had always envied the spirited mounts of the elegant Ladies who were usually attended by smartly dressed gentlemen, parading up and down Rotten Row.

They would stop only to talk to their friends who were driving in open carriages or walking along the paths.

She had never said so to her mother, but she had often longed to be one of the girls in the carriages whose parents seemed to know everybody who was riding or driving.

They made the Park seem like an intimate Reception Room, but she and her mother never met anybody they knew.

Isla thought her mother looked just as beautiful as, in fact more beautiful than, most of the Ladies of Fashion.

It seemed unfair that they should have so many friends and her mother so few.

Isla and Lord Polegate went from stall to stall until at

last he said it was time to return to the house because he wanted her to rest before dinner.

"We are going to dine early, my dear," he said, "then I want to talk to you about yourself."

"I am afraid that is a very dull subject," Isla replied. "It would be much more interesting to talk about you."

Then, because it had been worrying her, she said:

"I thought you would have ... friends staying with ... you ... Will they not be ... arriving in time for ... dinner?"

"The only person staying is yourself," Lord Polegate replied, "and that is exactly as I like it. One day I will give a party for you, but for the moment I want you all to myself."

She looked at him in surprise but thought she could hardly question what he meant by that.

Instead, she hurried ahead of him towards the house.

"I have already sent a message to Mrs. Blowfeld," he said when they reached the hall, "to find you something appropriate to wear tonight, and which will make you look even lovelier than you do at the moment."

"Thank ... you," Isla said shyly.

Then because she thought he was going to kiss her hand again she hurried up the stairs and along the wide corridor which led to her room.

There was a maid she had not seen before to help her out of her gown.

As it was obviously expected that she would lie down, she was not surprised when she was provided with a pretty lace-trimmed nightgown.

She put it on and got into bed.

Because she was tired after all the excitement of the night before and her anxiety about her father, she fell sleep.

                               *   *   *

When Isla awoke, two maids were carrying a bath into her room.

When they had filled it with hot and cold water from huge cans, she got out of bed.

The water was scented, and there were big Turkish towels which smelled of lavender with which to dry herself.

It was all very luxurious, and she thought she must remember every detail and tell her father because she knew it would amuse him.

When her bath was finished, Mrs. Blowfeld came in carrying two gowns.

"There's a choice, Miss," she said in her hard, frigid voice, "but I thinks His Lordship'd prefer you in white."

"That is very . . . kind of . . . you," Isla said in a small voice. "I do hope His Lordship's niece . . . or whoever it belongs to . . . will not mind my borrowing it."

Mrs. Blowfeld did not reply but made a sound that was suspiciously like a sniff.

Because Isla could think of nothing more to say, she let the maid bring her a silk chemise trimmed with lace.

It was so soft and attractive that she did not protest even though she thought she should have worn her own.

They then produced a pair of the finest silk stockings she had ever seen.

They were so transparent that she was afraid if she wore them she might tear them, and she said shyly:

"I . . . I think it would be . . . best to wear . . . mine."

"These are what His Lordship likes," the maid replied.

Isla thought it was a strange remark.

However, she did not say anything because her attention

was caught by a pair of pink garters with which to hold the stockings in place.

Made of the most expensive satin, they were embroidered with little hearts made of *diamanté*.

"They are very pretty!" she exclaimed.

"They were all made by hand, Miss," one of the housemaids explained.

"It seems a lot of work for something which is never seen?" Isla laughed and did not realise that the housemaids exchanged glances.

They then produced, instead of a whalebone crinoline, as she had expected, two petticoats that had frill upon frill of expensive lace from the knee to the ground.

She realised they constituted a frame for the gown.

When the housemaids held it out, it certainly looked very much more elaborate than anything she possessed, or her mother.

There were frills of silk edged with very expensive shadow lace and a bertha of the same lace, but very much deeper, embroidered with pearls.

Isla looked in the mirror and, knowing she would never afford anything so expensive, she exclaimed involuntarily:

"It is beautiful and I promise I will be very, very careful with it."

"That'd certainly make a change, Miss," Mrs. Blowfeld said.

"A change?" Isla asked.

"Some of the young Ladies are extremely careless and after one of these gowns has been worn, it takes the seamstress a long time to repair it."

"How could they possibly be so careless with anything so pretty?" Isla asked, and did not see the expression in Mrs. Blowfeld's eyes.

She left the room to take away the gown that Isla had

not chosen and the housemaid, a middle-aged woman who was arranging her hair, said:

"You're very young, Miss. Does your mother know you're staying 'ere on your own?"

"My mother is dead," Isla replied, "and my father is very ill."

"And there's nowhere else you could go?"

"I wanted to be in London so as to be near my father," Isla explained. "But now His Lordship wishes to stay until tomorrow."

She was facing the mirror, and she looked up and saw the housemaid's face behind her.

She noticed that the woman pressed her lips together as if to prevent herself from saying something.

Almost as if she knew what she was thinking, Isla said:

"It does seem strange to stay without any luggage, but when His Lordship asked me to come to the country, I thought it was just for the drive. I had no idea I would be staying here for the . . . night."

"I thinks, Miss, you'd have been better off in London!" the housemaid remarked.

There was something in the way she spoke that made Isla long to ask her why, but at that moment the House-keeper came back into the room.

"If you're ready, Miss," she said, "I think 'Is Lordship's waiting for you downstairs."

Isla got to her feet.

"Then I must not keep him waiting, must I? Thank you very much for helping me."

She turned to the housemaid and added:

"And thank you for doing my hair. It was very kind of you."

She moved to the door, and as neither of the women

spoke, she started down the corridor. As she did so, she heard the housemaid say:

"If you asks me, it's a cryin' shame! She's too young!"

Isla slowed her step.

She wanted to go back to ask the housemaid what she meant, but as the Housekeeper was there, she doubted if she would tell her.

As she went down the stairs, she was puzzling over what she had heard, and also about the young Ladies who had worn the gown she was wearing in the past and been so rough with it.

It certainly seemed in perfect condition, and she thought perhaps the Housekeeper was just exaggerating and disliked having to lend it to her.

Lord Polegate was waiting in the same room in which they had drunk the champagne when they arrived.

He was wearing evening-dress, but he did not look as smart or as dashing as her father.

She thought, in fact, that it made him look even older than he did in the daytime.

He stood watching her as she came towards him.

When she reached him and dropped him a curtsy, he put out his hand to take hers, saying as he did so:

"That is how I wanted you to look—and that is how you are going to look in the future."

She made no comment, and he said:

"I have a surprise for you. We are not going to dine in the large Dining-Room, but in the smaller one, which I use sometimes when I am alone. Come! I will show it to you."

He slipped her hand through his arm and drew her away from the Salon down a long passage at the end of which there was a small Dining-Room.

Isla thought it far more comfortable and congenial than the one in which they had eaten at luncheon.

There was a small round table in the centre decorated with flowers, and there were candles which lit the room.

There was something intimate and at the same time attractive about it.

It looked, she thought, rather like a stage-set she had seen in one of the Plays to which her mother had taken her.

Lord Polegate insisted on her having a glass of champagne, but she did not really want it.

He drank several glasses himself before they sat down at the table.

Dinner was brought in with only two servants instead of the four there had been at luncheon.

"Now, as I shall ring the bell between the courses, we can talk to each other," Lord Polegate said. "It is impossible to talk with servants listening to every word."

"What does it matter if they do hear what we say?" Isla asked.

"When I make love to you, I have no wish for an audience," Lord Polegate replied.

She looked at him in surprise, and when she saw the expression in his eyes, she said quickly:

"That is . . . something you . . . must not . . . do!"

"Why not?"

"B-because . . . we have only just met . . . and . . ."

She was about to say "You are too old," then realised it would seem rude.

Instead, she changed it to:

"You know . . . nothing about me."

"I know everything I want to know," Lord Polegate said. "You are not only the most beautiful person I have ever seen, but also the most enchanting!"

His voice deepened as he went on:

"You have captivated me, and I am going to make you very happy and very comfortable in the future."

"I am very . . . happy with . . . Papa."

"But your father is ill; in fact, he may be laid up for a long time, so naturally I have to look after you."

It flashed through Isla's mind that if her father was ill for a long time, there would be no money coming in.

Although the Benefit might pay off a number of outstanding bills, there were still others, and she had left herself only a few pounds for everyday expenses.

"We can talk about that later," Lord Polegate said quickly. "Now I want you to enjoy your dinner."

It was an excellent meal, but Isla was beginning to feel frightened.

She was very innocent and unaware of the danger she was in.

At the same time, she did not like the way Lord Polegate spoke to her, or looked at her, and she was worried by his compliments.

When friends of her father's had come to the house, they had paid her mother exaggerated compliments.

Yet they had not spoken in the same way as Lord Polegate did.

Nor did they look at her until she felt almost as if she must cover her breasts with her hands.

Because he had no wish to frighten her, he talked to her, as he had at luncheon, of other things.

Nevertheless, all the time she was aware that he was watching and appraising her.

She felt her fear growing so that it seemed to move through her body until it reached her throat.

When dinner was finished, Lord Polegate drank his glass of port and said:

"Now I have a surprise for you! I am sure it is something that is quite unique to this house, which you will never see anywhere else."

"What is it?" Isla asked uncomfortably.

He rose from his seat and, going to the panelled wall beside him, he pressed his fingers against a piece of the carving.

To her astonishment, a panel flew open to reveal a small staircase twisting upwards.

"A secret staircase!" she exclaimed. "How exciting! I have often heard about them, especially in houses that belonged to the Royalists when they were fleeing from the Cromwellian troops."

"The house was unfortunately not built in that period," Lord Polegate replied. "This is a little innovation of my own. And now I want you to climb up and see what you will find at the top."

Because she was interested, and it was certainly better than listening to the strange compliments Lord Polegate paid her, Isla negotiated the narrow staircase.

He followed, and as she had the uncomfortable feeling that he might be looking at her ankles, she hurried.

At the top she found there was another panelled door, which was open.

She slipped through it and found herself, to her astonishment, in her own bedroom.

It was the last thing she had expected, and yet there was no mistaking the ornate furniture, the draped bed, and the cupids round the mirror.

"Does that surprise you?" Lord Polegate asked behind her.

"It is . . . my bedroom."

"Of course it is," he answered. "Is it not clever of me to think of such an amusing way of going to bed?"

He had shut the secret panel behind him and came towards her, saying:

"You must admit, Isla, I have been very patient, but

now I want to kiss you, and to teach you, my beautiful little Lady of the Picture, about love."

As he spoke, Isla suddenly realised that this was what she might have anticipated, and she had been very stupid.

She backed away from him, saying:

"No . . . please . . . you must not do that!"

"Why not?"

"Because as I have already told you, we do not . . . know each . . . other."

"I know everything I want to know, and as I find you the most fascinating person I have seen for a very long time, I cannot allow you to escape me!"

Isla gave a little cry and ran away from him to the other side of the bed.

"Please . . ." she said, "you must not . . . look like that . . . and you . . . should not be . . . here in my bedroom. . . . I know Papa would not . . . approve."

"As your father is incapable of looking after you at the moment," Lord Polegate answered, "you must allow me to take his place."

There was silence while Isla stood with the bed between them as if it were a protection, her eyes on his face.

She did not quite understand what he intended, but she was frightened—very frightened.

"You have to trust me," Lord Polegate said, "to look after you, and it is something I shall enjoy doing."

He walked a little nearer to her as he said:

"You shall have the most beautiful gowns that are obtainable, I shall cover you with jewels, and you shall have your own carriage and the finest horses I can buy. What is more, Isla, when I have finished teaching you about love, you will find it very enjoyable."

"I . . . I do not know what . . . you are . . . saying," Isla said desperately, "and I do not . . . want these things . . .

from you! I know it is . . . wrong of you to . . . offer them . . . to me."

"Wrong? It is never wrong for a woman to be dressed as befits her beauty, or to be housed in a fitting frame."

He sat down on the bed and leaned towards her as he said:

"I refuse to allow you to live in that pokey little house from which I collected you. I have one in St. John's Wood, which is infinitely preferable and where you shall have your own maids. Come along, Isla! Be sensible, and realise what I am offering you!"

There was a little silence while with a courage which seemed to come from without rather than within her, because she was so afraid, she replied:

"I think . . . what you are . . . offering me . . . My Lord, is . . . something wicked . . . and which would . . . shock Mama and Papa . . . if they knew about it."

Lord Polegate's lips twisted as if he were amused at what she had said before he replied:

"I think you have forgotten that if, as I suspect, your father is in debt—and what actor is not?—and will not be working for some months, you will find it difficult to live without food."

He had a smirk on his face as he continued:

"And as he has kept you a secret for so long, I doubt if you have many friends."

"I can . . . look after . . . myself," Isla said bravely.

"I think that is very unlikely, and anyway, I intend to look after you!"

He rose from the bed and came slowly round to where she was standing on the other side of it.

"Now, be sensible, my dear," he said.

He put out his hands to catch hold of her, and she gave a little scream of horror and pulled herself away from him.

He hung on to her bertha, and she heard it tear as she ran to the other side of the room.

It was then, as if the mists that had covered her mind had cleared, she understood what the Housekeeper had meant when she said the gowns had been torn.

She knew the stockings and the pink garters were what "His Lordship liked."

She knew, too, why the housemaid had said it was a "crying shame, and she was too young."

As it came into her mind, she wanted to scream and go on screaming.

Then, as he came slowly towards her, she realised, and it accentuated her horror, that he was enjoying her resistance.

He was stalking her as a man might stalk a wild animal, certain in his mind that his "prey" would not elude him.

He was in no hurry, and there was a smile on his thick lips which told her he was very sure of victory and that she could not escape him.

She tried to scream, but now she felt that she must faint because it was impossible to breathe.

Then she told herself she would not give in so easily. She must fight, fight him until she died of horror.

He had come nearer, and instinctively she backed towards the wall behind her.

As she did so, she pressed against something hard and realised it was the door-knob.

She was trembling so violently that it was hard to think; and yet, as she stared at him, and her eyes seemed to fill her face, he stopped.

"I want you, Isla!" he said. "And I intend to have you! You may fight me, but I shall win!"

His voice seemed to ring out, then he said in a quiet, almost hypnotic tone:

"Come to me, I will make you come to me. It would be a pity to spoil that very pretty gown."

From the way he spoke, Isla was certain it was something he had said before.

Now, facing him, with only a few feet between them, she thought frantically of what she could do, how she could save herself.

"Help me . . . Mama! Help . . . me!"

She felt her prayer was a desperate cry for help, and if it failed, she would have to go to him as he commanded.

Then in a voice that did not sound like her own, she said:

"Y-you . . . make me . . . shy because you are . . . looking at me. Turn round . . . and perhaps I will . . . obey you."

He gave a little laugh, and it was the sound of a man who had attained his objective.

"Very well," he said, "come to me of your own free will and you will never regret it."

He turned round as he spoke, and with the swiftness of a deer Isla turned the handle of the door.

She had a moment of fear that it might be locked, but the key was on the inside and the door opened.

She slipped through it, slamming it behind her, and started to run.

She raced down the stairs.

There were two footmen in the hall, and by the greatest good fortune the front-door was open, as two more footmen were rolling up the red carpet which had been laid on the steps.

She sped out through the door almost before they realised she was there, and then she was running down the drive quicker than she had ever run before.

She thought when she had gone a little way that she

heard somebody shouting behind her, but she did not stop to look.

She only ran on, knowing that if she were recaptured now, there would be no hope of escaping again.

She was breathless by the time she reached the wrought-iron gates which were half-open, and sped through them out onto the road.

She had noticed when they arrived from London that Lord Polegate's entrance was on the main road and not in the village as she had half-expected.

Outside, she looked from right to left and saw in the distance a carriage approaching, drawn by two horses.

Without thinking, she ran towards it down the centre of the road.

chapter five

THE Marquis of Longridge, driving home, heaved a sigh of relief that dinner was over.

It was, in fact, the most boring meal he had eaten for a long time, but he thought with satisfaction that he had achieved what he had set out to do.

He had known that the Lord Lieutenant, Lord Middleborough, intended to retire at the end of the Summer.

He had been extremely apprehensive in case Lord Polegate was recommended for the position rather than himself.

As the owner of the largest acreage in the County, and head of a family that dated back for five-hundred years, he was the obvious successor to represent Her Majesty.

It was well known, however, that the Queen preferred Lord Lieutenants to be married men, and, if possible, on the way to middle-age.

The Marquis did not qualify in either of these respects.

But he knew that if he had the support of the present Lord Lieutenant, who had been a great friend of his father's, it would influence the Queen.

In any case, Lord Polegate was unpopular in the County.

The Marquis had played his cards very carefully, and when the Ladies left the Dining-Room, he had quickly led the conversation round to the Lord Lieutenant's resignation.

"We shall miss you," he said, "although I feel the work involved has become too much for you."

"That is true, my boy," the Lord Lieutenant said, "and the Queen has most graciously expressed her regret that I can no longer carry on."

There was a pause. Then the Lord Lieutenant said:

"You know, Welby, that as I was so devoted to your father, I would like you to take my place."

"I should be very honoured to do so," the Marquis said respectfully.

"The difficulty is," the Lord Lieutenant went on, speaking very slowly, "that you are not yet married, and the Queen is always afraid that younger men, especially those as handsome as yourself, might become involved in a scandal in one way or another."

The Marquis drew in his breath. This was what he had expected.

"I know I can trust you," he said in a low voice, "not to let this go any further except at your discretion, to the Queen, but I am, in fact, hoping to be a married man sometime next year."

The Lord Lieutenant started.

"I had no idea of this!"

"It has to be kept a close secret," the Marquis said,

"owing to mourning, so I know you will not speak of it unnecessarily."

"I understand, my dear boy, of course I understand," the Lord Lieutenant answered, "and this will make things very easy. I should have been extremely upset if that damned fellow Polegate had stepped into my shoes!"

"And so should I!" the Marquis said. "He is a bounder of the first water!"

"Nevertheless, he covers his tracks very cleverly," the Lord Lieutenant said, "and, of course, he is married, although his wife, being a sensible woman, has as little to do with him as possible."

He gave a short laugh, which made him cough before he added:

"He excuses her absence by saying that she suffers from ill-health, which I imagine is true enough, seeing she is married to him!"

He laughed again and repeated some rather unpleasant rumours that were circulating about Lord Polegate's behaviour.

The Marquis was barely listening.

It was now, as he was driving home, that he wondered where he was going to find a wife by the New Year.

By that time, if he had been appointed Lord Lieutenant, there was little anybody could do if he remained a bachelor.

At the same time, he disliked lying on principle, and in any case, he was getting to an age when he knew it was important for him to have an heir.

Moreover, if he was to take not only the Lord Lieutenant's place but other positions at Court, a wife could be useful.

Unfortunately he found it impossible to think of any woman who was unmarried and the right age.

This was not surprising, considering he spent his time

with the sophisticated, witty and alluring Beauties who had made London the envy of Europe.

There was no doubt that the parties given for and by the Beauties were extremely enjoyable.

Unfortunately, however, the Ladies in question were all married.

The Marquis could not even think of a widow who would grace the end of his table and the family jewels.

'Where will I find a suitable wife?' he asked himself as the horses travelled swiftly through the dusk.

He thought he would be wise to tell his oldest sister of the problem when she next came to London.

Suddenly he became aware that his horses were slowing down.

He thought it must be some rural reason, like a straying cow or sheep which had escaped from a field onto the road.

The carriage came to a standstill.

He could hear the voices of the coachmen, then the door was opened and his footman said:

"Excuse me, M'Lord, but there's a young woman who insists on speaking to Your Lordship."

"What does she . . ." the Marquis began.

Before the footman could reply, somebody had slipped by him, and a very young and frightened voice begged:

"Please . . . please . . . take me away . . . anywhere . . . just away from here . . . as . . . quickly as . . . you can!"

The Marquis stared at the newcomer in amazement.

By the light of the candle-lantern fixed to the front of the carriage he could see two very large and frightened eyes and a small white face framed with fair hair.

He was aware that the young woman was wearing an evening-gown, which was unusual on the High Road at this hour of the night.

Then, as he was about to speak, she looked over her

shoulder, gave a little scream, and climbed into the carriage.

"Hide me . . . I beg of you!" she pleaded. "They will . . . take me back to him . . . and he is . . . wicked and . . . evil!"

As she spoke, the Marquis realised that a footman in livery had appeared from between the wrought-iron gates a little way down the other side of the road.

It was then he was aware they belonged to Lord Polegate.

The girl flung herself down on the floor at his feet, and making up his mind characteristically quickly, the Marquis said to the footman:

"Drive on!"

The door was shut, and the footman climbed back up onto the box.

As the wheels started moving, the girl on the floor of the carriage bent forward to hide her face as if she were afraid she might be seen.

As they drove past Lord Polegate's entrance, the Marquis was aware that the first footman he had seen had been joined by another.

They were looking up and down the road as if in search of someone.

When the horses were a little farther on, the Marquis said:

"It is safe now. I suggest you sit beside me and tell me what all this is about."

The girl raised her head, and now that he could see her more clearly, he was aware that she was very lovely.

In fact, she was so beautiful and so obviously a Lady that it seemed extraordinary that she should be running into the middle of the road pursued by Lord Polegate's footmen.

The Marquis put out his hand to help her onto the seat beside him, and realised as he touched her that she was very cold and trembling.

He had a feeling that she was so frightened that her teeth were almost chattering, and he said in a calm, rather dry voice:

"I hope you will tell me what has happened to you."

"I . . . I managed . . . to run away!"

"From Lord Polegate?"

She gave a little shudder and said in a voice that was slightly inarticulate:

"H-he was . . . horrible . . . and I am . . . frightened . . . very frightened of h-him!"

"But you are staying with him at his house!"

"I thought . . . I was only . . . driving down . . . from London . . . for luncheon . . . and returning . . . afterwards."

The Marquis did not speak, and Isla went on:

"How could I have guessed . . . how could I have imagined that he would behave in . . . such a . . . wicked . . . shocking manner?"

"You must have had some idea what he was like," the Marquis said. "You have only to look at him to see that he is a Roué."

"I only . . . saw him for the . . . first time this . . . morning . . . when I was worrying about . . . Papa."

As she spoke, Isla made a little sound that was almost a cry as she said:

"What . . . shall I . . . do? Papa is lying ill in his . . . house and if I go back . . . I will . . . meet him again. . . . I cannot . . . bear it . . . I cannot!"

She sounded so frightened that the Marquis felt not only bewildered but also intrigued.

"Suppose you start at the beginning," he said gently. "First of all, tell me who you are."

"My name is Isla Kenway."

He made no comment, and after a moment she said:

"My father is Keegan Kenway . . . you may have . . . heard of him."

"Of course I have!" the Marquis answered. "But I had no idea he had a daughter! Are you also on the stage?"

"No . . . of course not! Mama would have been . . . very shocked at . . . the . . . idea! But I felt . . . there was nothing . . . else I could do . . . last night."

"What did you do?"

Slowly, and with some difficulty because Isla was so frightened that she was almost incoherent, the Marquis managed to extract from her the whole tale of what had occurred.

He found it all incredible.

He had always thought Keegan Kenway must be the sort of raffish character he depicted so brilliantly on the stage.

That he should have hidden away a daughter who had never until last night seen him on the stage was hard to believe.

Yet the Marquis, who was always prepared to be cynical and certainly critical, found it difficult not to think that every word Isla told him was the truth.

She was so obviously genuinely disturbed and horrified at Lord Polegate's behaviour, he was sure she was as innocent as she appeared to be.

He realised as she told him exactly what had happened that she had not even now fully realised what Lord Polegate had intended.

She only had an idea that the clothes she was wearing had something to do with it and that he intended to kiss her and keep her with him during the night.

Isla certainly had answered the Marquis's questions as clearly and, he thought, as truthfully as she could.

But she was shocked and bewildered, and when she told him how she had managed to get away, she said:

"But . . . Papa is in his . . . house in London . . . How can I go there . . . if Lord Polegate is . . . waiting for . . . me?"

Her fear made her tremble, and the Marquis answered:

"I suggest that you come back to my house and we will plan what you must do."

As he said the word "house," he saw Isla look at him quickly, and he thought, questioningly, and he therefore added:

"In case it sounds a little unconventional, let me assure you that my grandmother is staying with me at the moment. She is very old, and therefore will have gone to bed before dinner."

He knew Isla was listening, so he continued:

"But she still constitutes a chaperon, which you tell me you were expecting to find when you drove down with Lord Polegate."

"I know Mama would not have . . . expected me even to . . . have luncheon alone with a man," Isla said, "but he insisted that . . . we should go driving . . . and I thought as he was . . . so old . . . it would not . . . matter."

The Marquis smiled to himself, knowing that Lord Polegate would not find this very complimentary, but he merely said:

"I see no alternative for tonight but for you to stay as my guest at Longridge Park."

"It is . . . very kind of you," Isla murmured, "and I am very . . . grateful. But tomorrow . . . if you can . . . arrange it . . . I must go . . . back to London."

There was silence. Then she said in the frightened voice she had used in the first place:

"You do . . . not suppose . . . Lord Polegate will come to my . . . house looking for me?"

"I should imagine," the Marquis replied, "if his servants

have been unable to find you lying in a ditch, that is the first place he will look."

"Then . . . what can I do?" Isla asked. "What . . . can I do?"

"I will think of something," the Marquis said. "In the meantime, I think you must be brave and, unless you want a great deal of talk, it would be best to say as little as possible in front of the servants."

She drew in her breath, and he thought that she braced her shoulders before she replied:

"Yes . . . of course . . . and I am very sorry if I . . . sounded hysterical."

The Marquis thought she had every excuse for being hysterical after what she had just been through.

He had heard before of Polegate's penchant for very young girls, and there had been whispers amongst the servants in the village that he dressed them up.

No one, of course, was supposed to know of their existence.

Yet, as the Marquis knew, everything that happened in the country was carried on the wind, from cottage to cottage, door to door.

If Polegate thought his behaviour in his wife's absence went unnoticed, he was very much mistaken.

As they drove on, the Marquis from his corner of the carriage was unobtrusively watching Isla.

He thought that actually, considering what she had been through, she showed an exceptional self-control.

Most women, he was quite sure, would have been screaming and crying buckets of tears at their plight.

Once he had reminded her to be brave in front of the servants, she had gripped her fingers together and raised her chin in what he could consider only an admirable manner.

He knew she was worrying as to how she could reach her father without encountering his host.

The problem, the Marquis thought, was certainly a difficult one, and he could not for the moment think of a solution.

He knew he had to try, not only in order to save a frightened, unhappy girl, but also because he actively disliked Lord Polegate.

Ever since he had inherited his title and estate from his father, who had been too good-humoured to quarrel with anybody, he had found that Polegate, whose boundaries marched with his, was objectionable.

He was very rich and pushed himself forward in the County, where they accepted his donations and his charity simply because they needed the money.

At the same time, most people kept Lord Polegate at a distance and laughed behind his back at his ambitions to be more important than he was.

Where the Marquis was concerned, it was a question of Lord Polegate's game-keepers quarrelling with his and arguing over the accepted boundary lines between their two estates.

There was also the jealousy of an older man for one who was younger and of greater social importance.

The Marquis had, in fact, for a long time tried to dismiss Lord Polegate from his mind.

It was only when the question of the Lord Lieutenancy came up that he promised himself that Polegate would attain it only over his dead body.

He thought now, with Isla trembling beside him, that here, if necessary, was a story by which he could destroy Polegate's attempt to shine in the County.

One whisper from him, amd what had occurred tonight would make every decent woman sweep her skirts aside and refuse every invitation which came from Polegate House.

The Marquis, therefore, was prepared to welcome Isla as his guest with open arms.

They arrived at his very impressive ancestral home which had been added to and refronted by the Adam brothers in the middle of the eighteenth century.

When Isla stepped out of the carriage, he was startled when he heard her give a little gasp.

He thought perhaps she was feeling pain.

Then he realised that she was staring up at the pillared entrance, with its long stretch of stone steps, an almost incredulous expression on her face.

"What is it?" he asked.

"Your house . . . it is so . . . magnificent! Exactly what I had always . . . hoped to see."

He was surprised at her reaction, not because it was unusual, but that she should feel like that at a moment when she had so much else to occupy her mind.

He realised when she entered the hall that she was looking round her with an expression of admiration.

The Marquis walked into the very attractive Drawing-Room, which opened out of the hall.

The candles were alight in the chandeliers, and again he saw Isla look round her appreciatively.

"What would you like to drink?" he asked. "I think it would do you good to have a glass of champagne."

"No, no . . . please . . . not champagne!"

He had a feeling, although she did not tell him so, that she was thinking of the champagne she had drunk with Lord Polegate.

"A cup of coffee or perhaps some chocolate?" he said to the Butler, "and I will have a brandy."

"Very good, M'Lord!"

The Marquis turned from giving the order to look at Isla clearly for the first time.

He realised as she stood almost in the centre of the Drawing-Room under one of the great chandeliers that she was so lovely that he thought he must be dreaming.

How was it possible that he could pick up in the road anything so exquisite?

Then he was aware that her eyes were still frightened.

When she sat down on the edge of the sofa as if her legs would no longer support her, her hands were trembling.

Until that moment her thoughts had been diverted by the size and beauty of his house.

Now the problem of what she should do was again in the forefront of her mind.

As the Marquis looked at her, he felt he could read her thoughts.

"Do not worry," he said. "You are quite safe, and tomorrow we will decide what we can do about your father."

"I have just . . . remembered that I have . . . no clothes," Isla said, "except what I am wearing . . . and they belong to . . . Lord Polegate."

"Then what I will do," the Marquis said, making up his mind, "is to send a groom first thing in the morning to Polegate House to ask for your own gown. At the same time, the groom can return what you are wearing now."

Isla considered this for a moment. Then she said:

"You . . . you do not think . . . Lord Polegate will . . . make you . . . send me back?"

"That, I assure you, is something I would not do in any circumstances," the Marquis said definitely. "He has behaved disgracefully, as I am sure your father will tell you when he is well enough, and the best thing you can do is not to worry about him any further."

"But . . . I cannot . . . help it!" Isla said.

There was silence, then she said in a rather different tone of voice:

"I must tell you . . . I have . . . no money with me . . . for my fare to London."

The Marquis smiled.

"I was not thinking of sending you in a stage-coach, nor do I expect you to pay me for your accommodation to-night!"

There was a note of laughter in his voice, and Isla smiled at him as if she had been very stupid.

Then she said:

"I was not meaning exactly that. It is just that I feel so . . . helpless. I realise now it was very, very foolish of me to have allowed Lord Polegate to take me driving, but it seemed rude to refuse."

"It is something you will have to learn to do in the future," the Marquis said a little dryly.

He was thinking of Isla's beauty and her way of looking so helpless and pathetic that every man she met would want to help her.

He knew that sooner or later they would frighten her.

"I tell you what I will do," he said little later when Isla was sipping the hot chocolate which had been prepared for her by the Chef.

She looked up at him expectantly, and he said:

"First thing tomorrow morning, as soon as it is light, I will send my Secretary to London to find out how your father is. He will get there before Lord Polegate returns and, if he is better, perhaps we could move him to your own house without there being any trouble about it."

"Oh, could we do that?" Isla asked. "It is what I wanted to do all along, to look after Papa myself."

"Then that is what we will do," the Marquis said, "and

when you have finished your chocolate, I want you to go to sleep, and try not to worry about anything."

"I will . . . try," Isla said, "and, thank you very, very much for being so kind."

She paused before she added:

"Suppose you had . . . not come along the road . . . just then and they had . . . caught me?"

"But I did," the Marquis answered, "and I promise you on my honour that I will protect you from Lord Polegate."

Her eyes lit up for a moment, and he thought he had never known a woman in his whole life whose face was so expressive.

At the same time, she was so lovely, he thought when he looked at her that he must be dreaming.

He escorted her across the hall and up the magnificent staircase to where a maid was waiting to show her to a bedroom.

He thought she might have been a nymph who had slipped into the house from the lake, or an inhabitant from one of the stars who had come down to earth by mistake.

The housemaid was an elderly woman who had been at the Park since the Marquis was a small boy.

"I want you to look after Miss Kenway, Edith," the Marquis said. "Her clothes have been lost, unfortunately, but I am sure you can find her something to wear."

"Leave it to me, Master Wel—I mean . . . Your Lordship!" Edith replied.

The Marquis held out his hand to Isla.

"Edith will look after you," he said, "and try to sleep. Everything will seem better in the morning."

"That is what Mama used to say," Isla answered, "and thank . . . you again more than I can . . . possibly say in . . . words."

She made a little curtsy, and he stood watching her move along the passage beside Edith.

She moved so gracefully that her feet hardly seemed to touch the floor, and she floated as she walked.

Then he told himself it was a very unexpected ending to the evening.

He would certainly ensure that swine Polegate did not get his hands on the wretched girl again.

At the same time, as he went to his own room, he was wondering how it could be possible to remove Keegan Kenway from the house in Park Lane without there being a scene.

"I have to help her somehow," he told himself before he fell asleep.

*　　*　　*

To Isla's surprise, she slept far longer than she had ever slept in her life before.

It had taken her a long time to get to sleep.

She had first said a long prayer of gratitude that she had been able to escape from Lord Polegate.

Then she thanked God that the Marquis had appeared like a Knight in shining armour to save her just at the right moment.

"Thank You, thank You, God," she finished, "and, please, Mama, tell me what I should do."

She tried not to remember that if her father was not earning, there would be a great many expenses, and there was very little of the Benefit money left.

All that mattered at the moment, however, was that she had escaped from Lord Polegate.

The room in which she was sleeping was very quiet and nobody was likely to disturb her.

"What . . . time is it?" she asked when Edith brought in her breakfast.

"It's nearly ten o'clock, Miss."

"How can I have slept so late?" Isla asked.

"I 'spect you was tired, Miss," Edith said sympathetically, "an' it's a good thing you were not in a hurry to get up. All your things have arrived from Polegate House, and on His Lordship's instructions I sent back the white gown you was wearing."

"Thank . . . you."

She never wanted to see the gown again, and she hoped that Edith had also sent back the pink garters and the silk stockings.

She did not want to think about them, and if they were still here, she knew she would have them put in the dustbin.

It was an hour later before, dressed in her own gown, Isla went downstairs.

A footman informed her that the Marquis was in the Library, and she made her way there.

She opened the door a little shyly to find the Marquis sitting at his desk in the sunshine.

He rose to his feet as she entered and thought as he did so that Isla was even lovelier in the daylight than he remembered.

He had, when he awoke, thought that the whole episode must have been a dream.

Now Isla was very much alive, and, he thought, quite different from anybody else he had ever seen.

He found indeed everything about her incredible.

How could she really be the daughter of a Music Hall artist, however talented, and yet not only look and behave like a Lady, but be so innocent of the world that he thought it must be an act?

When Isla came into the room now, he thought that no actress could portray a girl who looked so shy, and at the same time entranced by her surroundings.

"I...I have been looking at your pictures as I came down the stairs," Isla said, "and I know Mama would have been thrilled to see them in their...right surroundings."

"What do you mean by that?"

"I have seen pictures like yours in the Galleries and Museums," Isla explained, "but in their right setting, they are far more impressive and far more exciting."

"I am glad they please you!" the Marquis said. "Now, sit down, Isla. I have something to say to you."

She did as he told her, and her eyes were apprehensive as she said:

"Have you...heard from...Lord Polegate?"

"I thought you might guess that he has written to me a very rude letter suggesting that as you prefer my company to his, you should remember he is looking after your father, and if he is moved precipitately and without due care from his house in Park Lane, it might result in his death!"

Isla gave a little cry.

"How can he...say things...like that?"

"I think he wrote to me in a temper," the Marquis said, "and I am sure he would not actually throw your father out without making proper provision for his welfare."

"I think I should...go back to Papa...at once!"

"And suppose Lord Polegate is there?"

He thought she went very pale as she said vaguely:

"He...he...could not...do anything to me in... London?"

The expression in her eyes was very moving, and the Marquis went a little nearer to her as he said:

"I promised that he should not hurt you, and that promise remains. And now I have a suggestion to make."

"What is it?"

"First sit down, then listen very attentively."

Isla obeyed him, and her eyes were on his face as the Marquis said:

"I am sure you have no wish, after what happened yesterday, for your father to accept Lord Polegate's hospitality. I therefore suggest that we take him away from where he is at the moment."

"I want to . . . do that!" Isla said. "But I am rather . . . afraid . . ."

Her voice faded away as if she could not put into words her fear that if she took her father home, Lord Polegate might come to their house.

Then there would be nobody there to protect her from him.

"What I am suggesting," the Marquis went on, "is that we move your father to my house which, as it happens, is only a little farther up Park Lane. You can stay there with your father, and I will arrange for somebody, perhaps one of my older relatives, to chaperon you."

Isla clasped her hands together.

"Do you really . . . mean that? How can . . . you be so kind . . . so unbelievably kind?"

There was a hint of tears in her voice, and the Marquis remembered that she had not cried last night, but now his kindness had touched her heart.

"What I have already done," he said, "is to send my Secretary early this morning to London to enquire how your father is, and also to speak to Sir Martin Simpson about him."

He paused a moment and then continued:

"He should return by luncheon time. Then we can decide how soon we can remove him, and whether there would be any danger to your father in our doing so."

Isla looked at him, and very slowly two large tears rolled down her cheeks as she said:

"I did not know that ... anyone could be so ... wonderful to me ... and to Papa."

"If you cry about it," the Marquis replied, "I shall be afraid I am making you unhappy!"

"I am so happy that I want to go on saying 'Thank you! Thank you! Thank you!'"

He smiled, and when she searched for a handkerchief and could not find one, he handed her one of thin lawn which bore his crest.

She wiped the tears from her cheeks and said:

"Perhaps Papa is better this morning and he could also thank you himself."

"I am sure we shall soon hear him singing 'Champagne Charlie' again with everybody singing along with him!" the Marquis said.

Isla gave him a brave little smile, and he went on:

"What I suggest we do now is to ask Edith to find you a riding-skirt which will fit you, and I will order the horses."

He saw Isla's face light up.

"Can we ... really do that? Can I really ... ride with ... you?"

"As soon as you are ready," the Marquis replied.

She gave a little cry of excitement, and without saying any more ran towards the door.

As she opened it she looked back and smiled at him.

Then, although he could hardly believe it was true, he felt a very strange reaction in the part of his anatomy he called his heart.

* * *

One-and-a-half hours later, riding back towards the house, Isla said:

"I have never enjoyed anything as much as riding one of your magnificent horses!"

She knew that Silverstone was not only magnificent, but also perfectly trained for a Lady.

She had been a little anxious that she would disgrace herself.

She had not ridden for some time, and her mounts had not been as spirited or as well-bred as the Marquis's.

But Silverstone carried her so perfectly that she had not had a minute's anxiety.

The beauty of the Park, the magnificence of the house, and the presence of the Marquis himself made her feel it was all unreal.

Yet it was the most thrilling thing she had ever done.

"How could all this have happened to me just because Papa is ill?" she asked herself.

Then she felt a little pang of anxiety in case he was not better, as she hoped, and would not be able to go back to the Oxford for a very long time.

"We will manage somehow," she reassured herself, but she knew it was going to be very, very difficult.

The Marquis's voice broke in on her thoughts.

"You are not to worry!"

"How do you know I am worrying?"

"Your eyes are very expressive, and I want you to be happy."

"I am happy, so very happy, and there are no words with which I can tell you so."

"I, too, enjoyed our ride," the Marquis said, "and if we have to go to London this afternoon, or tomorrow, I will drive you in my Chaise with the finest team of horses I have ever possessed!"

There was no reason for Isla to tell him how much she

looked forward to the experience; he could read it all in her eyes.

They rode back to the house, and Isla changed from the habit she had borrowed back into her own gown for luncheon.

She learned when she came downstairs that the Marquis's grandmother was not well enough to join them.

But she had sent a message to say she would like to meet Isla at tea-time, after her rest.

"I would not want to bother her," Isla said.

"She is longing to meet you," the Marquis answered. "I think she often finds life very dull living in the country."

"Does she stay with you all the time?"

"No, she has a house about ten miles from here on the estate, but at the moment I am making improvements to it, and I did not want her to be disturbed by the noise the workmen make."

"I can see you are not only kind but very considerate," Isla remarked. "Mama always said that kind men like Papa were very rare."

"Thank you for the compliment!" the Marquis replied.

Isla felt she had been rather forward, and blushed.

She had no idea how lovely she looked as she did so.

The Marquis thought for the hundredth time that she had a unique beauty that was very different from anything he had ever seen before.

They finished luncheon, which was delicious, and went into the Library because Isla wanted to see the books.

"Sometimes," she said, "when Mama and I wanted to look up the history of some particular picture, we used to go to the Library of the British Museum, and it was very exciting browsing through the books there."

"You can browse here as much as you like."

She threw out her arms as she said:

"I would like to read every book in your Library! I wonder how long it would take me?"

"Perhaps two to three hundred years!" the Marquis teased.

"Then I shall have to come here as a ghost!" Isla laughed.

He realised as she did so that she had a dimple he had not noticed before, and he thought the sunlight must have been caught in her eyes.

A footman came into the room.

"Excuse me, M'Lord, but Mr. Browning would like to speak to Your Lordship."

The Marquis left without any explanation and Isla was suddenly sure that Mr. Browning was the name of the Secretary who had gone to London to find out if there was any news of her father.

She waited a little apprehensively, standing at the window, looking out on the sunlit Park.

There were deer lying in the shadows of the great oak trees, and she thought how secure and happy they looked.

She heard the Marquis come back into the room, but she did not turn her head.

She was just tense, waiting to hear what he had to tell her.

He came and stood beside her, then unexpectedly taking her hand, he held it very closely in both of his.

"You have to be brave, Isla," he said very quietly.

She looked up at him and saw the answer on his face.

She gave a little cry even before the Marquis could say very quietly:

"Your father is dead!"

chapter six

WITHOUT thinking, without realising what she was doing, Isla moved towards the Marquis.

He thought she was about to faint and put his arms round her.

Then, as she hid her face against his shoulder and he felt her body trembling and was aware that she was fighting her tears, he knew incredibly that he had fallen in love!

He could hardly believe that what he was feeling was real.

Yet he knew he wanted to look after Isla and protect her, not only against Lord Polegate, but everything else in the world.

He stood holding her against him and knew that never in his whole life had he felt for any woman what he was feeling now.

It was not only that Isla was so unexpectedly lovely, and that she was innocent and unspoiled.

There was something deeper which made him recognise that she was unique.

At the same time, he could not help knowing that he could not marry her. Then he thrust the thought away and concentrated on her and what she was feeling.

"Your father is dead," he said very gently, "but he died as I would like to do when my time comes."

Isla did not answer, but he knew she was listening.

"My Secretary, Mr. Browning, found out from somebody who was at the party exactly what happened."

He felt Isla draw a little closer to him, as if, like a child, she wanted his protection and the feeling of security he gave her.

"It was a very amusing, very gay party which Lord Polegate gave at the Café Royale," the Marquis went on. "The food was delicious and, as you can imagine, there was a great deal to drink."

He felt Isla shiver, but she did not raise her head and he continued:

"They started proposing toasts and several famous actors who were there made short speeches in reply."

He felt Isla must know what was coming when he said:

"Then, when they toasted your father, everybody in the room shouted for him to sing 'Champagne Charlie.'"

As the Marquis spoke, Isla could hear her father singing the song as he had sung it when she was in the frame listening to him.

She remembered the lilt in his voice, the manner in which he seemed to galvanise the huge audience with his vitality.

"Your father sang the song they all loved," the Marquis was saying, "and they, of course, joined in the chorus."

His arms tightened as he finished.

"Your father drank down the glass of champagne he was holding, then he fell down onto the floor behind him."

"How . . . can it have . . . happened?"

Isla's voice was so low that the Marquis could hardly hear it, but he knew what she was asking.

"I think," he replied, "that it must have been the excitement of the whole evening, his and your success at the Theatre, and, of course, the way everybody complimented him at the party."

He prevented himself from adding that Keegan Kenway had also already drunk too much.

Instead, he said:

"Because he was unconscious, he really died in his hour of triumph, and no man could ask for more."

"I cannot . . . believe . . . it!" Isla whispered. "But now he will . . . be with . . . Mama."

"Of course he will," the Marquis agreed, "and I am sure they both know that I will look after you."

"Why . . . should you do . . . that when I am . . . a stranger who had . . . thrust herself on . . . you?"

The words were almost incoherent, and the Marquis did not answer.

Instead, with his arms still round her, he drew her gently to the sofa.

She sat down and he saw that she was very pale.

Her eyes had a stricken look about them, which he knew was due to shock.

It was not, however, the terror that he had seen when she had escaped from Lord Polegate, which he hoped he would never see again in any woman's face.

She looked at him for a moment, and he thought that no

one could look more in need of care and protection.

"I must . . . go to . . . London," Isla said, "and see about Papa's . . . Funeral."

"Let me do that for you," the Marquis said. "I am sure you do not want to go to Lord Polegate's house again."

He saw her shiver, and he said firmly:

"Leave everything to me. I know Sir Martin Simpson, and I will make all the arrangements with him."

Isla's eyes were on his face as he was speaking. Then she said:

"I should not . . . impose upon . . . you like this . . . but I do not know . . . what to do."

"Just leave everything to me."

The Marquis took her cold hand in his and said:

"I want you now to come and meet my grandmother, who I know will understand what you are going through. She lost her husband, whom she adored, and her favourite son was killed fighting in India."

There was silence, and he wondered if Isla would prefer to be alone.

Then with what he thought was a very commendable courage she said:

"I . . . I would like to . . . meet your grandmother . . . and thank you for saying . . . you will . . . see to Papa's . . . Funeral."

She hesitated, then added:

"It seems the . . . wrong thing to say at this moment . . . but it must not be very . . . expensive, as I have . . . so little money."

"I want you to leave that to me."

He felt her fingers tighten on his as she said:

"There is . . . no one else, and I am so . . . very glad I am . . . here."

He knew she was thinking that she might have been

120

with Lord Polegate when she learned of her father's death.

Then there would have been nobody for her to turn to, and no escape from his attentions.

He thought no other woman, especially one so young, could have been as brave as Isla for the rest of the day.

After she had sat with his grandmother and he had left them talking, he was surprised and relieved when Isla said she would like to join him for dinner.

He knew that most women in her place would be crying uncontrollably and wailing against Fate if they had been left alone in the world.

Moreover, where he was concerned, they would be making every excuse to cling to him, to cry on his shoulder, and expect him to comfort them in his arms.

He was intelligent enough to realise that to Isla he was not a man, but just something solid which she could hold on to for protection.

He realised, too, from what she had told him that she had never been completely alone before.

Although it seemed incredible, she appeared to have no relatives and no friends.

*　　*　　*

The Marquis slept very little that night, thinking of Isla and knowing he had not been mistaken in thinking that he loved her.

He was well aware that he should not only control his love, but, if possible, dismiss it from his mind and his heart.

It was inconceivable that a man in his position, with the prospect in a few months of becoming the Lord Lieutenant, should take as his wife the daughter of a Music Hall actor.

Isla was a Lady—there was no disputing that, but her father's notoriety on the stage would prevent her from being accepted in the Social World.

Certainly the doors of Buckingham Palace would be closed to her.

He knew the answer was quite obvious: it was what Lord Polegate had suggested and frightened her into running away from him.

The Marquis was therefore sure that was something that he could not suggest to Isla. But what was the alternative?

He tossed and turned in his bed, finally ringing for his valet at six o'clock.

Having ordered his horses, he left an hour later for London, first writing a short note for Isla and giving instructions that she was not to be called until she rang.

As he departed, although he was not aware of it, there was a grim look on his handsome face.

He was not looking forward to confronting Lord Polegate, as his journey might entail over the dead body of Keegan Kenway.

* * *

Isla again awoke late, which was not surprising, as she had cried herself to sleep.

Her mother had always said that it was extremely vulgar to cry in public.

She had therefore kept her tears until she was alone in the darkness of her bed, and no one could hear her.

She was sensible enough to realise that she was crying for herself more than for her father.

She believed absolutely that he was with her mother and they were now as happy as they had been before her mother had died.

She felt she could almost see them laughing with joy, forgetting that she was alone and lost in what was a frightening world.

When finally she rang for the maid who was looking after her, she found it was late in the morning.

It was a relief when she found a note from the Marquis, to know that he had gone to London.

Therefore she did not have to make a effort to go downstairs.

In fact, it was tea-time when finally she went down to the Library, thinking that to look at the books would take her mind off what had happened.

She did not like to think of what she would do in the future, or where she would live.

When she tried to remember the few friends who had come to the house, they none of them seemed the sort of people to whom she could turn for help.

"What can I do, Mama? What can I do?" she kept asking as she took down books from the shelves.

But when they were in her hands she found it difficult to concentrate on reading them.

Then at last the Library door opened and she knew the Marquis had returned.

He was looking, she thought, so strong, so kind and understanding, that without even thinking she ran towards him.

Only when she had reached his side did she bring herself to a stop and make him a little curtsy.

"You are . . . back! You are . . . back!" she cried.

The Marquis thought the relief in her voice was like the song of the birds.

"I am back," he said, "and I have a lot to tell you!"

Holding hands, they walked to the sofa and sat down side-by-side.

"Papa?" Isla said as if she were prompting him.

"I saw Sir Martin," the Marquis replied, "and everything is arranged for your father to be buried tomorrow."

He saw the expression in Isla's eyes and went on:

"It is unusually quick, but you will understand that Lord Polegate does not want him to remain in the house longer than is necessary. Sir Martin has therefore arranged for the Funeral to take place at St. Paul's, Drury Lane, which is in the Theatre World, and all his friends will wish to be present."

Isla made a little murmur, and the Marquis said:

"I do not want to upset you, Isla, but I think it would be a mistake for you to be present."

"But . . . surely I . . . ought to go to . . . Papa's Funeral?"

"Most of the people there would not know who you were, and there is no doubt that Lord Polegate will be there."

He saw Isla stiffen and said:

"Sir Martin told me he is making it into a big event as far as he is concerned, and is giving a huge luncheon when the Service is over."

"I . . . I cannot . . . meet him!" Isla said quickly.

"No, of course not!" the Marquis agreed. "That is why I suggest that you stay here, and as very few people are aware you are your father's daughter, no one will notice or be surprised by your absence."

Isla knew that was true.

Although she felt it wrong that she should not follow her father to his last resting-place, she remembered that nobody in the Theatre had known when her mother had died.

In fact, she and her father had been the only mourners in the Cemetery.

"You . . . are right," she said after a moment in a very low voice, "and I . . . will stay . . . here."

"What I am going to suggest," the Marquis said, "is that while we know that Lord Polegate is fully occupied with your father's Funeral and the luncheon, I take you to London and you can pick up everything you require from your house."

"I may . . . not go . . . back there to . . . live?" Isla asked.

"I think it would be a mistake, unless you wish to meet Lord Polegate again!"

"No . . . no! Of course . . . not! But . . . where am I . . . to go?"

"I am suggesting that you stay here while we think it over."

There was silence, and after a moment the Marquis said:

"I should be delighted to have you as my guest."

"But . . . you did not . . . know I existed until I . . . climbed into your carriage . . . and you cannot . . . want me now."

"Shall I say I do want you, and am very happy to help you."

He chose his words carefully and tried not to let his real feelings show in his voice.

"Did you . . . really mean . . . that?" Isla asked.

"I mean it, and I want you to be sensible and give us both time to find a solution to your problem. Nothing must be done in a hurry."

He thought as he spoke that when she knew him better, she might fall in love with him in the same way that he had fallen in love with her.

Then he almost laughed at his own thoughts.

Could he really be so unsure of himself, considering that for the last two years he had been pursued, enticed, and seduced by almost every beautiful woman he had met?

The Marquis was not a conceited man, but he would have been very stupid if he had not been aware that besides his title, his wealth, and his extraordinary good looks, he had also what people called "charisma."

It was something women always found irresistible.

Yet, at this moment he was very uncertain as to how a girl of her age, who knew nothing of the Social World, would accept his advances!

It was his instinct which told him he would have to tread very carefully.

Otherwise she would run away from him in disgust and horror, as she had run away from Lord Polegate.

There was no doubt that Isla was unique.

Although she was helpless, he was aware she had a quick brain and, surprisingly, was exceptionally well-educated.

He knew it was all these qualities that made her agree finally to everything he suggested.

It was not just because she felt helpless, but because, logically, she decided that what he proposed was the sensible thing to do.

They had dinner together, and when the Marquis set himself out to interest and amuse her, she responded with a courage which he admired more and more.

He was surprised to find how much she knew about Art and Architecture, besides being knowledgeable about the breeding of horses.

"How do you know about that?" he asked.

"Papa always took the Sporting Papers, because he said that the people in the Theatre bet on everything that moved!" she replied. "But because he sometimes had no time to read them himself, I used to read about which horses had won the Classic Races, and their breeding interested me."

"Also their owners, I suppose!" the Marquis said cynically without thinking.

Isla smiled.

"They were only names to me, but Papa had met quite a number of them."

By the end of the evening the Marquis was comparing Isla in his mind to a Madonna lily.

He thought it would be impossible for her to be so beautiful without having a character and a personality to match her looks.

He wanted to take her to Florence to see the paintings by Botticelli, of which she reminded him.

He wanted to compare her with the Greek statues in Rome and the figures on the Acropolis in Athens.

There were a thousand places against which he thought her beauty would stand out like a precious gem.

Then he was back with the same unanswerable question, which was what was he to do with her when they were back in England.

Before she went upstairs to bed, Isla said:

"I want to thank you, My Lord . . . but somehow there are no words . . . in which I can . . . do so."

She walked across the Drawing-Room as she spoke, to stand looking out into the darkness.

Because they had come into the room when the sun was still setting behind the oak trees, the Marquis had ordered the curtains not to be closed.

Now Isla, in the simple muslin gown which Edith had found for her to wear, lifted her head to the stars.

Watching her, the Marquis drew in his breath.

Every moment they were together he thought he fell more in love.

It was as if he were being tormented by a battle taking place between his brain and his heart.

"If I could . . . give you a . . . present," Isla said in her soft, musical voice, "I would take a . . . star out of the . . . sky and put it amongst your . . . treasures."

"But instead I am very content to have you among them!" the Marquis replied.

"I should be very . . . very honoured if you thought of me . . . as a . . . treasure . . . when you have so many and such magnificent . . . ones!"

It was almost a cue, the Marquis thought, to say what he really felt.

Then he knew that Isla was speaking quite impersonally.

She was comparing herself to one of his pictures or his collection of jewelled snuff-boxes which she had admired before dinner.

It never entered her mind that he desired her as a woman, or that she was anything more to him than an object of pity.

"Perhaps in time . . ." he reassured himself.

But now he was desperately afraid of moving too quickly and frightening her.

As a child, when he had tried to approach a fawn in the Park, he had learned that one quick movement or faint sound of his voice would send them scampering away.

It would take hours, perhaps days, before he could coax them back into trusting him again.

"What I want you to do is to try to be happy," he said aloud. "I know it is difficult, but everything that happens to us is an adventure, and that is the best way to think of it."

"Now you are talking just like Mama," Isla said. "She told me when I was very young that life was like the waves

128

of the sea—they come up—they go down—and we cannot expect everything to be smooth all the time."

"I can see your mother was very wise," the Marquis said.

"She taught me so many things and I missed her not only as a person when she died, but because she was so . . . knowledgeable."

"And you told me that you also learnt a lot at School."

"I learnt about places and people at School, but Mama taught me about . . . life."

The Marquis thought that was a very intelligent thing for Isla to think.

She had already told him that she had been to what he knew was a grand and expensive School, because his nieces were there.

He had been surprised that they had accepted Keegan Kenway's daughter, until a little shyly Isla had explained that she had been known by her grandmother's name of Arkray.

What was important, the Marquis thought, was that whether it was the School or her mother, her intelligence had been keenly developed.

She was also undoubtedly far better read than the older women with whom he had normally associated.

He had often thought, when he had not been making love to them, that their conversation was banal.

Talking to Isla, every subject they touched seemed to sparkle, and he thought he might have been with one of his men-friends.

Now, because he felt he could not look at her silhouetted against the light without taking her into his arms and kissing her passionately, he said:

"I think you should go to bed. I have to get up early, as you know."

"Of course . . . I should have thought of that!" she said. "How selfish of me!"

She turned from the window to walk towards him.

Once again the Marquis's self-control prevented him from begging her to stay and telling her how much he wanted her.

"Thank you . . . thank you!" she said as she reached him.

Then, as he put out his hand, she took it and curtsied; at the same time, he felt the softness of her lips on his skin.

For a moment he was still as he felt a thrill strike through his body like forked lightning.

Then she ran towards the door, opened it, and before he could move was running across the hall and up the stairs to her room.

* * *

Isla lay awake for a little while saying a prayer of thanks to God.

She tried not to worry about what would happen to her when the Marquis no longer wanted her here in his wonderful house.

"I must not become a bore," she told her mother, "and you have often said how people stay and stay and will not leave and that it is very bad manners to outstay one's welcome."

She told herself that perhaps she could find work of some sort, but she had no idea what that could be.

She was certain only that even if it meant starving to death, she would not go to the Theatre and meet men like Lord Polegate.

Edith called her in the morning and brought her breakfast to her in bed.

She was dressed in her own pretty gown and small bonnet five minutes before she had been told that His Lordship would be ready to leave.

Nevertheless, he was already in the hall as she came down the stairs.

She saw his Chaise outside and remembered he had promised he would drive his most outstanding team of horses.

They drove off, and as they went down the drive, Isla looked back at the house.

"What are you looking for?" the Marquis asked.

"It is so beautiful, and I am so . . . afraid I will not . . . see it . . . again."

"You are coming back this evening!"

"It . . . might be just a . . . dream."

"What do you mean by that?" he enquired.

"Everything that has . . . happened has been so . . . strange," she answered, "and I keep remembering . . . Papa's song and being afraid I will . . . wake up."

"I promise you that Longridge Park will be here when we return," the Marquis said with a smile. "If you would be disconcerted if it disappeared, think what I would be feeling!"

Isla laughed, and soon they were talking about the horses, and she forgot what had worried her.

They reached the little house in Chelsea in record time.

As the groom opened the door with the key which Isla had handed him, the Marquis said tactfully:

"I expect you would like to be alone while you sort out what you want to bring away with you. If there is too much for us to take, just leave it in a pile and I will send the servants with the Brake to collect it later."

He looked at his watch.

"It is now eleven o'clock," he said. "I will come back

for you at one, and we will go out to luncheon. Keep the door locked, and do not answer it to anybody but me."

Isla smiled at him, and as he drove off he thought he heard her bolt the door.

*　　*　　*

Alone in the little house, Isla felt it seemed so much smaller than she remembered, and she could hardly believe she had been away for such a short time.

Then, because she knew there was a great deal to be done, she went to her bedroom and began to pack the few gowns she possessed.

She had already told the Marquis shyly that she could not afford to buy any mourning.

He repressed a desire to tell her that he would pay for anything she wanted, and she said:

"Papa always hated mourning, and would not let me wear it when . . . Mama died. He liked bright colours, and thought that in black women looked like . . . crows!"

"I think the same," the Marquis said. "As you do not believe that your father and mother are dead, black would just be a waste of money, and who are you to impress by wearing it?"

"It is . . . so like you to . . . understand," she said.

It was, he knew, a compliment, and yet she spoke impersonally and would, he thought, have said the same to any other man who was with her.

When her trunk was full, and she had put in one or two of her mother's gowns because she knew they would fit her, she went to her mother's dressing-table.

She wondered if there was anything special she should take away with her.

She packed the silver hair-brushes and mirror which matched them, then opened the drawers.

She knew only too well that her mother had no jewellery.

The few pieces she had owned had been sold long ago to pay for her School fees.

She also knew that the small amount of money her mother had been left by the grandmother she had never seen had gone the same way.

There were a few handkerchiefs in one drawer which she put into the trunk.

Then, as she opened the other one she found, pushed right at the back of it, a large envelope.

She pulled it out and saw there was some writing on it. Then she read:

To Isla. To be opened in the event of my death and also that of Keegan Kenway.

Isla looked at it in surprise.

She wondered why she had never found it before, then remembered that it had hurt her so much to touch her mother's personal things.

She had therefore left everything just as it was after her mother died, and that was what her father had also wanted.

She thought at first that it was very remiss of her not to have found the envelope.

Then she realised it was only now that her father, too, was dead, that she was entitled to open it.

Carefully she slit it open and drew out the contents, which seemed so thick that at first she thought it must be a book.

But it was, she discovered, a letter written in her mother's beautiful, clear handwriting. She read:

My darling, precious little Isla,

I am writing this because I do not feel well, and I am afraid that if I die, you will never learn the truth, but I would not wish you to know it until your father, too, is dead.

It would hurt him so much, and I want you always to love and respect him, as you do now.

I want you also to love me, and not be shocked or angry when I tell you what I have kept secret for so long.

Isla drew in her breath, and for a moment she was afraid to go on to the next page.

What could her mother be going to tell her?

She was at first frightened, then, as she read on, incredulous.

Her mother had written very vividly. In fact, as she read and went on reading, it seemed to Isla that it was not a true story, but that she was immersed in the plot of a novel.

Her mother, she learned for the first time in her life, was the daughter of Major Bruce McDonald of the Cameron Highlanders and his wife.

She was their only child, and they lived in Edinburgh where, after a few brief postings abroad, he became Adjutant at Edinburgh Castle.

Bruce McDonald had married the daughter of Sir Robert Arkray, who lived outside Edinburgh, and their daughter, Janet, as she grew up, had many friends in the City.

Because she was so pretty, she was constantly entertained by the families of all the important personages in Edinburgh and in the surrounding countryside.

When Janet was eighteen, at one of the Regimental reunions which took place every year, the guest of honour was the Earl of Strathyre, who had served in the Regiment when he was a young man.

He came down from the North, and there was first of all a Reception given for him at which he met the wives and children of all the serving officers.

In the evening there was a dinner-party, and a Ball afterwards, at which all the Highland Reels were most skilfully danced.

Janet attended both engagements.

Before the Earl left Edinburgh for his Castle in the North, he had fallen in love with Major McDonald's daughter and asked her to be his wife.

Because it was such a brilliant marriage socially, it never seemed to strike anybody that a man getting on for fifty was not a suitable bridegroom for a very lovely girl of just eighteen.

Janet was, however, married to him and went North to the Earl's estate, which was on the borders of Sutherland and Caithness.

Nine months after the marriage she had presented her husband with the son and heir he had always longed for.

The boy was christened Iain, and for a short time he interested his father as much as his fishing and shooting, which filled his days to the exclusion of all else.

It never struck the Earl that since he entertained only men of his own age as guests and his Castle was in a particularly barren and isolated part of the Highlands, life was exceedingly dull for his young wife.

It was five years later, when his second child was born, a daughter who was christened Isla, that Janet rebelled.

Her daughter's birth had been a difficult one, and she

felt she must get away from the gloomy Castle and the eternal conversation about sport.

With some difficulty she persuaded her husband to allow her to visit her parents.

Although they had come North twice to stay with her, she had never been allowed to return to Edinburgh with them.

Leaving Iain in the charge of a very capable Nurse, who had looked after him ever since he was a baby, she took Isla with her, because her parents had never seen her.

Only when she arrived in Edinburgh did she realise how much she had missed the company of young people of her own age!

Also she had enjoyed the dances which took place every week, the Concerts and Theatres that were available every night.

As Isla turned the pages, she could almost feel her mother's excitement and realised how enchanting everything had seemed.

The letter continued:

> I suppose, when I went to the Theatre to see *Hamlet*, it was inevitable that I should fall in love with Keegan Kenway!"

As she read the words Isla gave a little gasp.

It seemed impossible that her father was not Keegan Kenway, but was, in fact, the Earl of Strathyre!

Her mother went on to describe how handsome Keegan Kenway was, and also, although he was an actor, it was inevitable she should meet him.

He was the son of the Provost of Edinburgh.

He had started his Theatrical career when as a choir-boy

he had such a beautiful voice that people went to the Cathedral just to hear him.

The applause he received at the Church Concerts made him decide that however much his father and mother might oppose it, he would go on the stage.

When a distinguished Company of Players next came to Edinburgh, he begged them to take him on tour with them, and they agreed.

Within three years he was noted as one of the outstanding young British actors on the stage.

When, at thirty, he met Janet, he was already a Star whom people paid to see whether he was playing Shakespeare or some successful Melodrama.

Janet then wrote:

The moment I saw him, I fell in love with him, and he with me. We were both old enough to know what we were doing, and that is why you have to forgive me, darling, when I tell you that we ran away together, and that nothing else seemed to matter.

It was inevitable that Janet's parents would be deeply shocked at her behaviour, and so were Keegan Kenway's.

It had never struck Janet that she should return her daughter to her husband.

She had left him her son, and that should be enough, while she felt that Isla, because she was so tiny, needed her.

It was not long before Keegan Kenway had established himself on the London stage.

Because he was so happy with Janet and they were afraid that somebody might find out she was the Countess of Strathyre, they lived very quietly and secretly.

Only very rarely, after they had been together for some years, did they dare to appear together in public.

There was no reason for anybody to suspect they were not married, since Edinburgh was a very long way from London, and the Earl of Strathyre's Castle even farther.

Only when Isla grew older was her mother perturbed that she could have no friends, and that was when she decided she must go to School.

She told the Headmistress that she had married the son of Sir Robert Arkray.

There was no reason why the Headmistress should not accept what she was told.

Isla read on to the end of the letter.

That is my story, my darling, and I want you to forgive me for depriving you for so many years of what should have been your rightful place in Society, although I doubt if you would have found it very enjoyable, living in the far North.

If, when you read this letter, I am dead, and so is Keegan, whom you have always known as your father, then you must go at once to your real father.

He is a kind man at heart, and I do not think he will refuse to take you in, and perhaps he has missed you, although he has had your brother, Iain, with him.

It may be impossible for you to go alone to the North of Scotland. I therefore want you, when you have read this letter, to call at Strathyre House in Park Lane.

It was shut up all the time I was with your real father and I suspect he is unlikely to have opened

it now, but there are caretakers installed and you must ask them to help you.

I am sure your father's Solicitors, whose name I have forgotten, will have a branch of their firm in London. If not, you can stay at the house.

Write to your real father, tell him who you are, and I am sure something will be done for you.

Forgive me, my precious, but when you fall in love you will know that love is greater than anything else in the whole world and, when you find it, it is impossible to resist or refuse it.

I remain,

Your ever loving Mother,

Janet Strathyre

When Isla had finished reading the letter, she sat staring at it, finding it hard to believe that once again she had not been dreaming.

chapter seven

ISLA sat for a long time, just staring at her mother's letter.

This she knew was the answer to all that had been worrying her.

She had felt it was impossible to go on imposing herself on the Marquis, but at the same time she had no idea what else she could do.

Then like an answer to a prayer, her mother had solved the problem she had thought about over and over again.

She glanced at the clock and realised there was another half-an-hour before the Marquis returned as he had said he would, to take her out to luncheon.

She went down the stairs, sat at her mother's desk, and wrote a note to him.

My Lord,

You have been so kind and so wonderful to me in every way, but I have now found what I think will be somewhere where I will be safe, and no trouble to anybody.

I was so afraid you might find me an encumbrance but could not be rid of me.

Thank you, thank you, so very, very much! I shall never forget you, or your beautiful house.

Isla

Only as she signed her name did she remember how she had looked back at Longridge Park as they had driven away and thought it might vanish like a dream.

Now she knew that everything that had happened to her since she had gone on the stage in the picture had been a dream!

She was conscious as she wrote the Marquis's name on the envelope that she felt a strange heaviness like a stone in her breast.

She walked out of the front-door and hailed a cab, which, she was aware, would be waiting for a fare on the cab-rank at the end of the road.

As she did so, she knew she was intending to drive away to a new life and leave the Marquis behind.

"It is the ... only thing ... I can ... do," she whispered to herself.

A cab drew up outside the house and the driver obligingly said he would bring her trunk down the stairs.

She watched, saying goodbye as she did so, to all the years she had lived in the small house with her mother and Keegan Kenway.

It was also goodbye to the Marquis!

She had known him such a little time, yet he had filled her whole life.

"Be that everythin' yer wants, Miss?" the cabman asked, having heaved her trunk up onto the box.

"Yes, thank you," Isla replied.

She walked into the hall and picked up her bonnet from where she had left it on a chair.

Outside again, she shut the front-door, locked it, and put the note for the Marquis on the top step.

She knew in such a quiet street no one would remove it, and he would find it there when he returned for her in fifteen minutes time.

As the cabman drove on after she had told him to go to Strathyre House in Park Lane, she gripped her fingers together and stared ahead of her with unseeing eyes.

She was leaving the Marquis!

When she reached the North of Scotland he would never find her again and would soon forget her.

It was then, as the weight in her breast became a sharp pain, that she realised she loved him.

It swept over her like the warmth of the sun, then faded into a darkness in which there was no light as she realised that he was already consigned to the past.

She had lost her mother, Keegan Kenway, the life she had lived with them for so many years, and now the Marquis.

She wondered why she had been so foolish as not to realise she loved him when she was at Longridge Park.

She had thought riding beside him was the most exciting thing she had ever done.

Talking to him as they had last night was a thrilling experience which she could not describe even to herself.

She had been in love with him then!

She had, in fact, loved him when he had saved her from

Lord Polegate, taken her to his house and been so unbelievably kind and understanding.

"I love him!" Isla said, and remembered how her mother had written:

> **Love is greater than anything else in the whole world, and when you find it, it is impossible to resist or refuse it.**

"But I have to resist it because the Marquis does not love me," Isla told herself wistfully.

She had an impulse to turn the cab round, drive back, and be waiting for him when he arrived to collect her.

Why should she tear herself away from something that mattered to her more than love itself?

She knew, however, that it was her pride which told her she must not be an encumbrance on him.

He had picked her up off the road.

She was nothing to him and could play no part in the Social World in which he shone so brilliantly.

It was laughable how ignorant she was of everything that surrounded him and which he took for granted.

She thought of the many allusions which Edith and the other servants had made to the beautiful women who had stayed at Longridge Park.

They had suggested, without actually putting it into words, how much they had all loved the Marquis.

Isla could understand their feelings, but they at least had a chance of attracting him.

How could he possibly be interested in anybody as insignificant as herself?

No one indeed could have been more sympathetic over Keegan Kenway, or taken more trouble to save her from coming in contact with Lord Polegate again.

She had realised, however, that the Marquis had been willing to do this largely because he disliked Lord Polegate as a man and as his neighbour.

He was therefore in a way scoring off Lord Polegate by having rescued her from his odious advances.

"But how can I go on living on his charity?" she asked, and knew it was impossible now that she had an alternative.

It was, however, frightening when the cab turned into Park Lane.

Suppose the caretakers would not listen to her story of who she was?

Suppose after all these years the house had been shut up completely with no one living in it? Or, worse still, sold?

"I can always go back to the Marquis," she told herself reassuringly as the horses came to a stop.

The house certainly did not look deserted; the windows were clean and the brass knocker on the door was highly polished.

But as the cabman got down and raised it, she held her breath in case she was mistaken and there was no reply.

Then the door opened, and seeing a footman in a smart livery, she stepped slowly out of the cab.

Because she could see another footman in the hall, she thought that her father must have come South and was in residence.

The footman was looking at her expectantly and with difficulty she managed to ask:

"Please . . . c-could I . . . see the . . . Earl of Strathyre?"

The footman opened the door wider and asked:

"Will you come in, Ma'am?"

Isla turned to the cabman and said:

"Wait for me, please."

Then she entered the house.

The footman led her across the hall, and she looked at the polished but rather gloomy furniture.

Then he opened the door into what she supposed was the Library or Study.

There was a large flat-topped desk in the middle of the room, the walls were covered with books, and above the mantelpiece there was a fine picture of grouse flighting over the moors.

"What name shall I say, Ma'am?" the footman asked.

Isla hesitated.

"Will you tell His Lordship that somebody wishes to see him on a very important matter?"

The footman looked surprised, but apparently he was too well-trained to say anything and merely went from the room, shutting the door behind him.

Isla stood, too nervous to sit down.

She was not really capable of thinking about anything except that in a minute or two she would see her father.

Her mother's letter seemed almost too incredible to be true, and she now wondered if because her mother was ill when she wrote it, if she had imagined it.

She heard voices outside in the hall, and her heart gave a frightened leap as the door opened.

She was expecting an elderly man, but instead a tall young man, very smartly dressed, entered and walked towards her.

"You wanted to see me?" he asked.

"I asked . . . to see . . . the Earl of . . . Strathyre!"

"I am the Earl!"

Isla stared at him, and now she realised he was staring at her.

"Who are you?" he asked sharply.

It was impossible to speak. Her voice seemed to have died in her throat.

Then he said in an incredulous tone:

"Surely—because you are so exactly like—the portrait of my—mother you must be—Isla!"

"And . . . you are . . . Iain?"

He smiled.

"I have often wondered what you were like, and now that I see you, I think I should have recognised you even if we had met in a crowd."

"How . . . could . . . you have? . . . I mean . . . you knew about . . . me?"

"Of course I know about you," he replied.

"I had never . . . heard of . . . you until . . . half-an-hour . . . ago!"

He stared at her in astonishment, then he said:

"Sit down! This is the most exciting thing that has happened for a long time, and you must tell me why you are here."

Because it was so difficult to speak, Isla sat down in the nearest chair.

As if he realised she was shy, he asked:

"Is our mother with you?"

"Mama is . . . dead," Isla replied. "She died . . . more than a . . . year ago."

"Oh—I am sorry!" Iain exclaimed. "I have always longed to meet her."

"You . . . longed to . . . meet her?" Isla repeated.

Iain smiled again.

"My father never mentioned her name, but everybody else talked about her in whispers."

He laughed and went on:

"My Nurse told me what happened as soon as I was old enough to understand, and the other servants, the game-keepers, the gillies, and even my father's friends talked about her when they did not know I was listening."

"I . . . I had no idea . . . I was not . . . Keegan Kenway's . . . daughter," Isla said, "until . . . he died."

"I read in the newspapers this morning that he was dead," Iain said, "but it did not make any mention of his wife or family, and I wondered what had happened to my mother. I thought perhaps he had left her."

"No . . . they were very . . . very . . . happy," Isla said quickly, "and I think . . . it was due . . . to Mama that he was such a . . . huge success on the . . . stage."

"He was certainly very well known." Iain smiled. "They have heard of him even in the far North!"

"Why are . . . you . . . here?" Isla asked. "Mama wrote me a letter which you must read . . . telling me I was to . . . come here . . . as she thought there would be . . . caretakers . . . and . . . as I had . . . nowhere else to go . . . she thought they would help me to . . . go North to . . . find my . . . real father."

"I am sure he would have liked to see you," Iain said, "but he was too proud to admit to anybody what had happened. For a long time I think quite a lot of people believed that Mama was just staying in Edinburgh with her parents."

"When did . . . he die?" Isla enquired.

"Nearly two years ago," Iain replied, "and I think when our mother ran away he realised that one of the reasons was that she found it so dull at the Castle."

"Is that what . . . you find?" Isla enquired.

He shook his head.

"No, I love it! Although Papa sent me to School in Scotland, he let me go to Oxford, where I made a great number of friends. They come to stay in the Autumn, and I

148

have opened this house so that I can come here in the Summer."

"I wish . . . Mama had known . . . that," Isla said. "I am sure . . . she would have . . . liked to see you."

"And I would have liked to meet her!" Iain replied. "But as it is, I am very glad to meet my sister!"

"It seems . . . extraordinary that you . . . should know about . . . me . . . but I had never . . . heard of . . . you!" Isla remarked.

"Then we must make up for lost time," Iain said. "Are you going to stay with me?"

She looked a little shy as she said:

"M-my trunk is . . . outside on the cab."

"Then let us have it brought in!"

He rose to his feet and rang the bell.

The door opened almost immediately.

"Bring in Her Ladyship's luggage from the cab outside," he said, "and pay the cabman."

"Very good, M'Lord!"

As he finished speaking, he saw Isla's face and said:

"From the expression in your eyes, I have a feeling you did not realise that as my sister you must now take your proper place as Lady Isla McThyre."

"I . . . cannot believe it!" Isla exclaimed. "It is so . . . strange and so . . . incomprehensible . . . and I think the first thing you . . . should do is to read . . . Mama's letter."

She had put it into the bag she carried, and now she took it out and passed it to him.

"Thank you, but there is no hurry," Iain said. "I want to talk to you. I am finding it not only unexpected, but also delightful to realise what a very beautiful sister I have."

Isla blushed.

They talked all through luncheon, and during the afternoon.

Although the young Earl had intended to go out to dinner with some friends, he sent a message of regret that he could not be with them.

"I would . . . not want to . . . spoil your . . . fun," Isla said.

"You are not spoiling anything," he answered. "But I realise from what you have been telling me that you have a lot of enjoyment to catch up on."

She looked at him enquiringly, and he said:

"Perhaps like our mother you would have found the Castle rather boring. But now I have so many parties and so many friends in London that you are going to lead a very different life from what you have been doing all these years!"

"It sounds . . . wonderful!" Isla said.

At the same time, it occurred to her that perhaps at one of the parties to which her brother would take her she might meet the Marquis.

Underneath their laughter at so many things, she was still conscious of the heavy stone lying in her breast when she thought of him.

She wondered if he had been angry or glad when he found her letter.

"Perhaps it was rather rude," she told herself, "that I should . . . disappear so . . . quickly, but when he realised there is . . . nothing more he can do, he will . . . quickly forget . . . about me."

"Why are you looking unhappy?" Iain questioned.

She realised that her thoughts had carried her away from where she was in their conversation.

"I . . . I am just a little . . . bewildered."

"I think really you are looking back into the past," he said, "and that is something you must never do again."

"Never?"

"Of course not! We have to think this out carefully, and I decided when I was dressing for dinner that it is essential you should forget Keegan Kenway and pretend in the future you have never had anything to do with him!"

"How . . . can I . . . possibly do . . . that?" Isla asked.

"It is quite easy," Iain said. "Few people in the North and none here in London know that Mama ran away with him. There has never been a mention of it in the newspapers."

He paused to say slowly, as if thinking of each word:

"I think our story should be that you have been living quietly and alone with your mother in London, or anywhere else you like to name. It would be a brave person who had the impudence to enquire if you had anything to do with Keegan Kenway—the Music Hall actor."

Isla considered this for a moment before she said:

"I . . . see what . . . you mean."

"We can say that Mama is now dead, and you have therefore come to live with me, as you would have lived with Papa had he still been alive."

"I think they . . . must have . . . died at about . . . the same time," Isla remarked.

"I do not think you should go into those details," Iain said. "Just be very vague about it all, and people will be far too polite to ask personal questions."

"I hope . . . you are . . . right."

"What I intend to do now," her brother said, "is to take you to a number of parties in London so that you will meet my friends, besides being 'launched,' so to speak, into the Social World."

Isla gave a little cry.

"I am sure I will . . . not know . . . how to . . . behave!"

"There is no need to worry about that!" Iain said. "I will buy you some new gowns, and everyone will be too stunned by your looks to worry about anything else."

"I hope . . . you are . . . right," Isla said again.

"Everybody has always told me how beautiful Mama was. I have seen portraits of her, and you are exactly like her."

"That . . . makes me . . . very happy."

They talked after dinner until it was nearly midnight.

To Isla it was fascinating to hear about Scotland, how much her brother had enjoyed himself at Oxford, and all the plans he was making to modernise the Castle and this house in London.

"It is far too gloomy," he said. "You can help me choose bright-coloured curtains, and we will do up the Reception Rooms and have a Ball before the Season finishes."

"It all sounds very . . . very . . . exciting!"

At the same time, she knew that instead of meeting dozens of her brother's friends, she wanted to meet only one man.

When finally she went to bed it was in a heavily furnished, dull room which overlooked the small garden at the back of the house.

She was thinking of Longridge Park, and how beautiful everything had been.

Then she found herself crying, crying for the moon that was out of reach, the stars she could never take from the sky and give him.

"Why did I . . . have to . . . fall in . . . love?" she asked in the darkness. "Why could this not have . . . happened without . . . my meeting the Marquis and knowing no . . . other man would ever . . . touch my heart?"

She cried despairingly until she fell asleep from sheer exhaustion.

* * *

When Isla awoke it was quite late in the morning, and a well-trained maid brought her breakfast in bed and told her His Lordship had gone riding.

Isla was downstairs by the time Iain returned.

He came bursting in full of enthusiasm for a new horse he had just purchased which, he told her, was one of the finest stallions he had ever possessed.

"I am going to build up a decent stable," he said, "and, if I can afford it, have a few race-horses."

"I believe they are very expensive!"

"Papa was a rich man."

Isla did not say anything.

She thought of how she and her mother had to skrimp and save, and how frightened she had been that Keegan would not be able to pay his bills when she was looking after him.

As if her brother knew what she was thinking, he said:

"That reminds me—I have told my Secretary to order the best Dressmakers in Bond Street to call here immediately after luncheon. I have to go out, but I suggest you buy yourself a new wardrobe of clothes, and I expect you to look sensational in them!"

"You are . . . making me . . . nervous!" Isla protested, but he only laughed.

He disappeared after luncheon, but came back at about tea-time.

Isla had spent what seemed to her an astronomical amount of money on what she knew were the loveliest gowns she had ever thought to possess.

She and her mother had regularly pored over the *Ladies Journal* and they had also looked in the windows of the shops in Bond Street.

Isla therefore knew exactly what was fashionable and, thanks to her mother, had very good taste.

She was wearing one of her new gowns which had fitted her without alteration, and as Iain realised it, he said:

"You look lovely! Now I am going upstairs to make sure that you do not eclipse me completely!"

Isla looked at him enquiringly, and he explained:

"I am having a new kilt and evening-jacket made by the best Tailor in Savile Row. They told me when I arrived home that he was waiting for me."

"I shall enjoy seeing you in a kilt," Isla said.

"You will have to wait until we go to Scotland," Iain replied, "and then I promise you, you will be astounded by my magnificence as a Chieftain!"

They both laughed, and he went from the Library.

Isla walked across to the window.

There were thick velvet curtains, heavily tasselled, which she guessed must have been up for many years.

She was sure Iain was right to sweep away the gloomy furnishings which she was sure were echoed in the Castle.

It was probably the reason that her mother had longed for the gaiety of Edinburgh.

Now that she was alone again, it was difficult to think of anything but the Marquis.

Everything in his home had been so beautiful, so light, and certainly very different from the dark pomposity of Strathyre House.

She was half hidden by the curtains as she heard the door open and a footman say:

"If you'll wait in here, M'Lord, I'll inform His Lordship of your arrival."

She heard the door shut and realised somebody had been left inside the room.

Aware that the footman did not know she was there, and feeling it was embarrassing to hide herself, she pushed the curtains to one side and walked into the room.

Standing at the far end of it was a man, and at first sight of him she thought she must be dreaming.

It was the Marquis.

He was looking exceedingly smart, and seemed, because she had not expected him, to fill the whole room.

The movement she made in pushing aside the curtain made him turn his head, and when he saw her, he was as surprised as she was.

For a moment they were both completely still, just looking at each other.

Then with a little cry she could not repress, Isla ran towards him.

She did not know if he waited for her or if he moved towards her.

She knew only as she reached him that his arms went round her and without speaking he pulled her against him, and his lips were on hers.

He kissed her wildly, passionately, demandingly, and she knew as he did so that this was what she had wanted, cried and longed for, and now it had happened.

He kissed her until she felt as if she melted into him, and was part of him, and they were completely indivisible.

Only when they were both breathless did he raise his head, look down at her and then, still without speaking, he was kissing her again.

He kissed her now more slowly, with long, possessive, passionate kisses.

They made Isla feel that she must have died, because it was impossible to feel so ecstatically happy and still be alive.

She felt as if her whole body vibrated with inexpressible sensations that were like the glory of the sun, the music of the wind, and somehow, too, the roar of the waves.

Only when it overwhelmed her did she make a little murmur and hide her face against his neck.

"My darling, my sweet!" he said, and his voice was unsteady and a little incoherent. "How could you have left me? How could you have done anything so cruel and wicked as to disappear in that ghastly fashion so that I thought I should never find you again?"

"I . . . I thought you . . . would be . . . glad."

Her voice seemed to come from a very long distance away, but the Marquis heard it, and now he put his fingers under her chin to turn her face up to his.

"How could you think that?" he asked. "I cannot live without you, Isla! How soon will you marry me?"

He did not wait for her answer, but was kissing her again, kissing her in the same fierce, demanding fashion as he had done at first.

It was as if after being desperately afraid he had lost her, he was making her realise with his kisses that she was his, and nothing would ever divide them.

He felt her whole body quiver against him, and he knew that what she was feeling was what he was feeling too.

Only when the softness and sweetness of her lips beneath his told him that she surrendered herself utterly did he say:

"Now tell me you love me!"

"I . . . I love you!" she said. "I love you so much . . . that it was an . . . agony to leave you."

"Then why did you do so?" he asked angrily.

"I thought I was being a . . . nuisance and it was so . . . terrible to thrust myself . . . upon you without . . . any money."

"How could you leave me?" he asked again. "I read your note and had no idea where you had gone, or where I could find you."

As he spoke, as if for the first time, he began to ask why she should be there, and there was a horrified suspicion in his eyes.

Even as words formed on his lips, the door opened and Iain came in. Isla moved from the Marquis's arms with a little murmur of shyness.

Her brother came across the room towards them, holding out his hand.

"This is a surprise, My Lord," he said, "but I am delighted to see you!"

Then, before the Marquis could speak, Iain looked towards Isla and said:

"My sister has told me how kind you were to her after Lord Polegate behaved in that disgraceful manner."

"Your—sister?" the Marquis repeated, and there was no doubt he was stunned.

"My sister!" Iain confirmed. "Although we have not met each other for very many years."

"I had no idea!" the Marquis exclaimed.

"Nor had I!" Isla said.

She had moved back to his side, and now she slipped her hand into his.

The Earl looked from one to the other of them.

"Am I guessing correctly what has happened?" he asked.

"I have just asked your sister to marry me," the Marquis said, "and I think, though she has not put it into words, she has accepted!"

He saw the light in Isla's eyes and thought it impossible for anybody to look so radiant, so spiritually happy that she might have just come down from the sky.

He took her hand and kissed her fingers, and as he did so, Iain exclaimed:

"This is the most exciting thing that has ever happened, and we must certainly celebrate!"

He walked across the room to ring the bell. As he did so, the Marquis kissed Isla's fingers again.

"I do not understand," he said. "All I know is that I love you!"

"And I love you . . . too!" Isla said in a voice that only he could hear.

* * *

It was very much later in the evening before, after the Marquis had gone home and come back again to dinner with them, they finished talking.

There was so much to hear, so much to plan, and only when the Marquis went back to his home in Park Lane did he tell himself he was the most fortunate man in the whole world.

When he had read Isla's note and thought he had lost her, he knew that nothing else was of any consequence except that he should find her again.

Then he would keep her with him for the rest of their lives.

He had known that the Lord Lieutenancy or any other position he might occupy was of no interest to him beside the fact that he wanted Isla as he had never wanted a woman before.

She was everything he wished for in a wife.

He told himself that he would marry her even if it meant he had to lose most of his social friends.

If he had to spend a great deal of time in retirement in the country, every sacrifice would be worth it to hold Isla in his arms.

No one else would make him feel as she could.

He wondered frantically where she could possibly be, or what she meant by saying she had found somewhere where she thought she would be safe.

He had learnt while they were in the country how few people she had known in London, and she had actually said she had no friends to whom she could turn for help.

Then he went over every word they had ever said to each other.

He suddenly remembered she had told him that she had been at a School where they were very particular about the backgrounds of their pupils.

They accepted only the aristocracy and that was why she had been known as "Isla Arkray," after her grand-mother.

It had taken the Marquis a great many hours of despair during the darkness of the night to recall the name.

As soon as he did, he determined to visit the College of Heralds as soon as it opened the following morning.

The College of Heralds took a long time to discover what he wanted to know.

Finally they produced the Family Tree of Sir Robert Arkray, the last Baronet, who he learned had only one daughter, who had married a Major Bruce McDonald.

They had a daughter, Janet, who had married the Earl of Strathyre.

It seemed unlikely that this had any possible connection with Isla, but the Marquis was determined to leave no stone unturned until he found her.

He remembered he had met the present Earl of Strathyre, who was a pleasant young man, at Tattersall's, where they had been introduced and had discussed the merits of certain horses.

Then they had met a second time at the house of one of his friends.

Because Strathyre was not a familiar name in London, he had gone to see that friend to discover Strathyre's address, which he then discovered was not far from his own house in Park Lane.

"You did not expect to find me here?" Isla asked when he told her of his search.

"I had the idea that you would go to Scotland," he replied, "and I was quite prepared to follow you there."

"I hope you will both come to the Castle after you have finished honeymooning," Iain remarked. "The grouse should be very good this year!"

The Marquis's eyes twinkled.

"That is certainly something I must not miss!"

He looked at Isla as he said:

"I think, darling, we should go together, if it would not bore you."

"How . . . could I be . . . bored with . . . you?" she asked.

For the moment they forgot there was anybody else in the room except themselves.

"I refuse to wait a long time before Isla and I are married," the Marquis said to Iain a little later. "We want our wedding to be quiet, without hordes of people gaping at us and asking a lot of extremely tiresome questions."

"I am sure you are right," Iain agreed. "I suggest you get married quietly, have a glass of champagne here, and a cake if you like, then go off on your honeymoon."

"Shall we do that?" the Marquis asked Isla.

"Can . . . we?" she asked.

"It is what we are going to do," he answered, "and with your brother to give you away, you have nothing else to worry about."

"Now I am . . . sure I am . . . dreaming!" Isla whispered.

*   *   *

The Marquis and Marchioness of Longridge left Strathyre House with only the staff to throw rose-petals as they stepped into the Chaise.

The Marquis was driving, as Isla expected, his new team of horses, and she thought no man could look more handsome, more exciting, or drive with such expertise.

Before she left she had flung her arms round Iain's neck and said:

"You are the most marvellous brother I could ever imagine, and please . . . can we come to stay with you as soon as we come back?"

"I shall be waiting to welcome you with the Pipers in full dress," Iain replied, "so do not disappoint me."

"We will not do that, and I am so happy!" Isla smiled.

It was only when they had driven some way through the traffic that she asked the Marquis:

"Where are we going? I did not ask questions until now because I felt you wanted to keep it a secret."

"It is the last secret we will ever have from each other," the Marquis replied. "I am taking you to Longridge first to make sure it is not a dream, and the house is still there!"

Isla gave a little cry of delight.

"That is what I want more than anything else! Your house is so beautiful that I cannot believe it is to be my . . . home in the . . . future."

"And you will be the most precious treasure in it!" the Marquis said.

"You remember our conversation?"

"I remember everything we have ever said to each other," he answered, "but I have not yet had time to tell you how beautiful you looked as a bride."

He had, in fact, thought as she had come up the aisle of the Grosvenor Chapel in which they had been married that she was too beautiful to be real.

He felt she was some Divine creature who had come to him from the stars.

Then, as he felt her fingers tremble in his, he had known that he would look after her, protect her, and love her for the whole of his life.

She was everything he wanted, everything he had ever desired.

It seemed incredible that everything had gone so smoothly and so happily.

He had been prepared to marry Isla even if she had been known to be Keegan Kenway's daughter.

Yet he was aware what unpleasant things people would have said.

The manner in which she would have been treated by his relatives and the Society Women with whom he had spent so much of his time in the past would not have been pleasant.

He had been prepared to fight the world on her behalf, but now that was unnecessary.

Everything had been made easy because Isla was the sister of the Earl of Strathyre, the head of and the Chieftain of one of the oldest and most respected Clans in Scotland.

The Marquis was quite certain that he and Iain had arranged everything in such a manner that as far as Isla was concerned, Keegan Kenway would be completely forgotten.

The scandal which had been caused by her mother running away eighteen years ago would, as they had never subsequently been heard of together, die a natural death.

All that mattered, he thought as he drove on, was that Isla was now his.

Everything about her thrilled and delighted him, and every time he saw and touched her he fell more deeply in love.

They arrived in record time, and it was a wedding-present in itself that he should achieve it.

They drove down the drive and saw Longridge Park in front of them, the statues on top of the roof silhouetted against the sky, the windows gleaming in the sunshine.

Isla knew that once more she was stepping into a dream-world which was so perfect, so beautiful that she prayed she would never lose the enchantment of it.

As if the Marquis knew what she was thinking, he turned towards her and said softly:

"Welcome home, my darling!"

She smiled at him, then she said in a whisper:

"It is . . . true . . . really true that I am your wife . . . and this is now . . . my home as well as . . . yours?"

"*Our* home!" he corrected her. "A home that will always mean love and happiness for us, our children, and the generations that come after them."

He felt Isla press her cheek against his shoulder, and he knew she was moved by his words.

After they had dined quietly in the *Boudoir* which lay between their two bedrooms, Isla walked to the window to look up at the stars as she had done before.

The Marquis followed her.

"If you are still thinking of giving me a star as a present," he said, "it is something you have already done. You are my star, my precious, and you will guide and inspire me for the rest of my life."

"Can I . . . really do . . . that?" Isla asked, her lips raised to his.

"You can do it only if you are close beside me as you are now," he answered. "I do not want you in the sky, I want you, my darling, here with me, and closer still."

He gave a laugh of sheer happiness as he picked her up in his arms and carried her from the *Boudoir* into her bedroom.

The air was fragrant with the scent of flowers, and she saw, and knew it was on his orders, that the curtains were drawn back so that they could see the stars in the sky above.

He put her down beside the bed and removed the elaborate satin *negligée* trimmed with lace which she had worn during dinner.

She did not speak as he lifted her onto the bed and laid her back against the pillows.

She looked up at the sky remembering how she had thought that the Marquis, like the moon, was out of reach, yet she was now his wife.

It did not seem possible, but he was beside her, taking her into his arms.

"You are thinking of me?" he asked.

"How could I . . . think of anything . . . else?"

"I love you!" he said. "I love you so completely that I am jealous of your thoughts."

He paused to smile down at her, then continued:

"Just as I shall be jealous of anything which absorbs your attention, even the flowers, the woods, and the horses, if they keep you from thinking of me."

"They are all a . . . part of . . . you," she said softly, "all the things here which I have . . . never had in my life before, and . . . oh! . . . you . . . and you . . . and YOU!"

The way she spoke brought the fire into his eyes.

He looked down at her and thought she was so alluring, so exciting that he was half-afraid, as she had said so often, that this was only a dream.

Then he knew it was reality and he had to be very gentle, very controlled, and, as Isla had said, very kind, so that he did not frighten her.

Then, as their lips met, the sensations within them both mingled together and created an irresistible fire which neither of them could escape.

"I want you! Oh, God, how I want you!" the Marquis said. "But, darling, I am so afraid of frightening you, so that I might lose you again!"

"How...can I be frightened of...you...when I love you so that you...fill the...whole world?" Isla asked. "I thought you were like the...moon...out of reach...but now that I am...close to you...I know that anything is...possible...just because we are...together."

"You are right," the Marquis said, "anything *is* possible, and because you are part of the Divine, my whole life has changed."

"I want you...just as you are!" Isla whispered. "But I am...still afraid that I am...dreaming."

"We are dreaming together, but it is a dream that will go on and on and grow more intense and more beautiful because we will never wake!"

"You are...sure of that?"

"I will make you sure of it!" he answered.

Then he was kissing her beguilingly, wooing her with his kisses.

He kissed her eyes, her lips, the softness of her neck, then her breasts.

As she felt the starlight in the sky invading her body, she knew that just as she would guide and inspire him, he would be everything that was safe and secure to her.

"We are . . . one person," she thought.

Then as the Marquis went on kissing her, and his hand was touching her, she felt the starlight turn to flame, and her dream came true.

They were one person in mind, in heart, in soul, and—in body.

They were part of the Divine Love which was theirs for all Eternity.

Barbara Cartland, the world's most famous romantic novelist, who is also an historian, playwright, lecturer, political speaker and television personality, has now written over 460 books and sold over 500 million copies all over the world.

She has also had many historical works published and has written four autobiographies as well as the biographies of her mother and that of her brother, Ronald Cartland, who was the first Member of Parliament to be killed in the last war. This book has a preface by Sir Winston Churchill and has just been republished with an introduction by Sir Arthur Bryant.

Love at the Helm, a novel written with the help and inspiration of the late Admiral of the Fleet, the Earl Mountbatten of Burma, is being sold for the Mountbatten Memorial Trust.

Miss Cartland in 1978 sang an Album of Love Songs with the Royal Philharmonic Orchestra.

She has broken the world record for the last twelve years by writing an average of twenty-three books a year. She is in the *Guinness Book of Records* as the best-selling author in the world.

She is unique in that she was one and two in the Dalton List of Best Sellers, and one week had four books in the top twenty.

In private life Barbara Cartland, who is a Dame of the Order of St. John of Jerusalem, Chairman of the St. John Council in Hertfordshire and Deputy President of the St. John Ambulance Brigade, has also fought for better conditions and salaries for Midwives and Nurses.

Barbara Cartland is deeply interested in Vitamin Therapy and is President of the British National Association for Health. Her book *The Magic of Honey* has sold throughout the world and is translated into many languages. Her designs "Decorating with Love" are being sold all over the U.S.A., and the National Home Fashions League named her in 1981, "Woman of Achievement."

In 1984 she received at Kennedy Airport America's Bishop Wright Air Industry Award for her contribution to the development of aviation; in 1931 she and two R.A.F. Officers thought of, and carried, the first aeroplane-towed glider air-mail.

Barbara Cartland's Romances (a book of cartoons) has been published in Great Britain and the U.S.A., as well as a cookery book, *The Romance of Food*, and *Getting Older, Growing Younger*. She has recently written a children's pop-up picture book, entitled *Princess to the Rescue*.

In January 1988 she received "La Médaille de Vermeil de la Ville de Paris." This is the highest award to be given in France by the City of Paris.

In March 1988, Barbara Cartland was asked by the Indian Government to open their Health Resort outside Delhi. This is the largest Health Resort in the world.

Barbara Cartland was received with great enthusiasm by her fans who also fêted her at a Reception in the city and she received the gift of an embossed plate from the Government.